Jože Mlinarič was born in Slovenia. Since he was eight years old, he knew that he was a writer. In that period he started to write his first novel with a pretty adult theme about pregnancy problems in a young family. He didn't finish that novel. During schooling he wrote some poems, but he postponed serious work till a later time when he would have more life experience. His first novel came after his stay in Cyprus in 2000, the second in 2013, *The Last Man* in 2021. He tried to publish his novels, but was unsuccessfull until the 2021 when he met this publisher in the UK.

To my family and to all mankind.

Jože Mlinarič

THE LAST MAN

AUSTIN MACAULEY PUBLISHERS™
LONDON * CAMBRIDGE * NEW YORK * SHARJAH

Copyright © Jože Mlinarič 2022

The right of Jože Mlinarič to be identified as author of this work has been asserted by the author in accordance with sections 77 and 78 of the Copyright, Designs and Patents Act 1988.

All rights reserved. No part of this publication may be reproduced, stored in a retrieval system, or transmitted in any form or by any means, electronic, mechanical, photocopying, recording, or otherwise, without the prior permission of the publishers.

Any person who commits any unauthorised act in relation to this publication may be liable to criminal prosecution and civil claims for damages.

This is a work of fiction. Names, characters, businesses, places, events, locales, and incidents are either the products of the author's imagination or used in a fictitious manner. Any resemblance to actual persons, living or dead, or actual events is purely coincidental.

A CIP catalogue record for this title is available from the British Library.

ISBN 9781398483828 (Paperback)
ISBN 9781398483835 (ePub e-book)

www.austinmacauley.com

First Published 2022
Austin Macauley Publishers Ltd®
1 Canada Square
Canary Wharf
London
E14 5AA

I would like to thank my parents, my ancestors, my friends, but most of all my family and my patient wife, Maja, who has always supported me.

A big thank you to my good friend and companion, my spirit, who is guiding me on this exciting exploration of the mysteries of the Universe.

The number of days I have left in this world has long since been counted. I don't even know what day it is, or even what month, year 2034? I don't know; it doesn't matter. I don't know how many days I have left. I don't know how much longer I'm going to be sentenced to solitary exile. Before I join my loved ones and friends who have gone before me, I want to write down what I want to tell you.

Who am I writing to, I wonder? There's probably no man left in the world who hasn't become a robot and could read my writing. Maybe in a thousand years or more, an autonomous thinking living being will reappear and will be able to read what really happened to planet Earth, because the official history will be written by the masters and will be completely different from what actually happened on this planet. Even if no one reads my writings, I am sure that the messages synthesised by my mind and my spirit will go out into the universe, into the universes, into infinity. Maybe it was meant to be; maybe the universe decided our fate, maybe the Creator Himself. Or it is all due to the free will of individuals, which we sold for thirty gold coins. Free will, whether we were free to think at all, to decide. We were just meek sheep when they took us to the slaughter. We did not raise our eyes; we did not open our mouths when we were being shorn, and so all the way to the end, when we were taken to the slaughterhouses. We were born for them, we were educated for them, we lived for them, and we died for them. When they talked about freedom, they were actually talking about slavery. We were slaves, willing slaves, until we became useless eaters. They kept us alive as long as we were useful to them. When we became old jades, they let us out to graze on the poisonous grass.

Those who resisted them were destroyed, declared insane, unfit, the worst enemies. They have been excommunicated from society, from their society. Free will was just a dusty artefact from another time, from another world. If you wanted to exercise your free will, you were immediately killed, imprisoned; expelled east of their paradise. Some have consoled themselves that the spirit is free. The spirit is free, but it is chained and imprisoned in the body, and the mind is too weak to support the spirit, so it too is subdued.

I wonder if I did the right thing in rebelling against the masters, against the system, against the whole world, against fate. It would be better to put a bullet in your head or hang yourself from an apple tree in your home garden. But I did not have the strength, the courage to do such an extreme act. Taking your own life? Sometimes I really thought about that possibility, but deep down I always knew I would never do it.

I have no right to take what is not mine. I did not create myself and my life. My earthly life is not my property, and I have no right to destroy what someone else has created. Whether the owner of my life is God, or the owners of my life are my parents, who made me out of atoms and breathed life into my body, is irrelevant. It doesn't matter if I came into this world deliberately and with a purpose, or whether I was merely an unwanted product of my parents' sex. If I had a choice, I would not have chosen to live on Earth, at least not at this time when God has raised His hands and left us to Satan, or he did.

Maybe by writing this I can finally make peace with myself and with the Creator and prepare myself for the inevitable. What awaits me then, over there, behind the wall, behind seven high mountains and eight deep waters, I do not know. Maybe I'll continue my life on another planet, maybe I'll meet acquaintances in Dante's Inferno, maybe I'll become a deity, and maybe I'll just decompose into organic fertiliser for the vegetation around me. I cannot know, I can only believe. What to believe, what to believe in. If there is a God, why has He forsaken us? Why has He left us to the devil?

Our Father, Who art in Heaven…Just in case, I prayed the Lord's Prayer. It can't do any harm, as my mother used to say.

God was invented by the devil to conceal his true face so that the sheep would follow him unquestioningly. The devil is the alpha and the omega. He is the master of the universe, the dictator, the manipulator. He is a venomous snake that feeds on our souls. The soul comes into the world pure and free, but is immediately enslaved by the devil, who grows it according to his own standards, his own requirements. He raises us to be slaves, working in his garden, on his animal farm. The devil certainly exists, but God…?

Light and darkness, plus and minus, day and night, sun and moon, sweet and bitter…God and the devil. There must be a God out there somewhere. Without light there is no darkness, without day there is no night, without God there is no devil. Who is in charge, who is senior?

I have a hunch that it is Him, even though I am still not entirely sure because He keeps eluding me. Because the devil has conquered the world, because he has let so many people die, because he has allowed the horned man to subjugate everything and more. I want to hold God's hand, to touch His cloak, to feel the security of being with Him. Maybe there's refreshments waiting for me at the end of the road. Why at the end, why not at the beginning, in between?

Life is a race over hurdles, whether you beat them to reach the finish line, or whether you give up at the first, second or penultimate hurdle. And the winners should be rewarded; everyone who reaches the finish line and overcomes all the obstacles will be rewarded. That's what they say. My faith is still too weak. Will I finally wash my soul with this story and prepare it for the path ahead?

Part 1

1

I had a great time in Geneva. As an independent and freelance journalist, I could afford to work in locations where, as well as writing, I was fascinated by my surroundings. The place where I was currently staying was definitely high on the list of places I could live in one day. Or so I thought at the time.

The warm spring sun warmed me with its rays and filled me with the energy and optimism I needed after a long winter in cold Trondheim, Norway. Long, too long nights and too many days with no sunshine have drained me.

I came to Switzerland for CERN. My client wanted a series of articles from the European Organization for Nuclear Research. That was my area, an area bordering on science fiction, bordering on the twilight zone, the zone far away from everyday life. CERN was certainly a Mecca for adventurers like me, who were more likely to fly intergalactic spacecraft than walking on Earth. I enjoyed it and made money. What a beautiful life, La vita e bella. I am satisfied, but at the same time, I have kept my feet on the ground, because in this unpredictable life things can turn upside down very quickly. Bono sang it's a beautiful day to me. I ordered another beer and resumed what I had started as soon as I sat down in the sun-drenched garden of the pub by Lake Geneva.

I was observing my surroundings, and above all I was observing the people who were walking past me, each with their own thoughts, their own goals. I had a flirtation here and there with an interesting woman passing by. I was a man, a free hunter. I was not tied down. My work demanded me, and there was no room for a life partner, for children, for days that bored me. I loved children, I loved them very much, but I didn't want to have any of my own, not yet. There were so many things to explore, so many places to visit, so many adventures to have, so I hadn't planned my escape from the crazy world. I was crazy enough to live in a crazy world. I thought then that one day, there would come a day when I would have enough of everything and want to calm down, when I would get tired of airports, planes, hotels, motels, short-term rentals, Airbnb, tents, when I would get tired of people and adrenaline-fuelled days, when I would get tired of picking up my dirty underwear and taking them to the public or hotel laundry, when I would get tired of transferring my luggage from the car to the airport trolley, from the airport luggage cart back into the boot, when I'm old, incontinent and enfeebled, one day. Maybe I'll live until I become old, or maybe not, I thought. I didn't worry about it as long as I was alive, as long as I wouldn't vegetate. And if I were destined to be old in a normal world, Geneva would surely be one of the most sacred places suitable for my oldness.

When I came back from Norway, I stopped for a few days at home, in Slovenia. "Where are you going again? You've just arrived," my mother asked me.

I had to go and leave my mother. She wasn't too old yet, she was over sixty, and she knew how to enjoy life. At home, I met up with Beti, and she was still waiting for me. I told her to go, let her live her life. But she waited, she waited for me. Was that love, I wondered. She was in love with me, but I wasn't in love with her, at least I didn't think I was. It wasn't love. Every time we met I said to her, "Beti go, leave me alone." The years will pass and you will be left alone because of a vagabond like me. Nevertheless, I loved seeing her, I loved being with her when I was at home. Actually, Beti was always my first thought when I headed home. And Beti was waiting for me. Was that the much-vaunted love?

"May I sit down?" A blonde woman in her thirties, in my connoisseur's estimation, interrupted my mental wandering. Attractive, and with all feminine attributes, and very pleasant in appearance.

"Of course, please sit down," I replied in English, even though she had spoken to me in French. My French was like Allo, Allo French, so I didn't want to take a chance with it and drive this interesting creature away from me. I thought she had come to me because of me. After carefully checking the neighbouring tables, I realised that she had come to me because of the free chairs around my table, because I was alone. But she still came to me; maybe she likes me, or finds me likeable or interesting. If she disliked me, she would not have come to my table. Just as I opened my mouth to ask her if she lived in Geneva, another blonde woman came to the table. They hugged and kissed. The kiss was suspicious to me; there was too much passion in it for just plain friendship. They were holding hands. Nothing will happen, I told myself, drinking a beer and looking aimlessly at the space in front of me. As befits a true investigative journalist, I kept a close eye on what was happening at my table. I decided not to leave them; I would stay until they are gone. I hoped it wouldn't cost me too much beer, and as a result, I would be overwhelmed by a strong drunkenness.

As soon as the table to my left was cleared, a tall, grey-haired man, with a striking and incredibly symmetrical bald spot on the top of his head, wearing glasses framed by a gilded and thin metal frame, with a large eagle nose, smoothly shaved cheeks and beard, dressed in a dark grey suit, a white shirt, and a dark tie around his neck, sat down there. He looked at me. When I met his eyes, he quickly looked away from me. He was nervous, his eyes darted back and forth, he shifted restlessly in his chair and in his nervousness, which was very obvious and disturbing, he inadvertently banged his head on the tray on which the waiter had brought him the coffee he had ordered. The cup flew off the tray and shattered on contact with the ground into dozens of pieces, which settled in a brown puddle. The waiter had to change his shirt and trousers. The grey-haired man was loudly apologising and waved his hands around, and pushed the glasses case off the table which had fallen at my feet. I bent down and picked it up off the floor. A clumsy neighbour also leaned down, and bumped his head to my head. He said nothing, looked at me with frightened eyes, took the case from my left hand and dropped a small piece of paper into my palm, which I clenched into a fist. He got up and hurried towards the bar. After a few moments, I opened my hand on my left thigh and unfolded a crumpled piece of paper with a note on it:

Rue de Berne 21, 3rd floor,
At 20. 00
There is a sign on the door "Private"

What does this mean? Does the stranger know I'm a journalist and has something to say to me, or is this an indecent invitation from an older married man, I wondered. On his left hand, a wide wedding ring glittered. Does this old man think I am gay and a seller of my body? This gay reason was the most plausible to me. I was increasingly convinced that it was an indecent invitation. Nobody knew me there. In CERN, I have only been in contact with the spokesperson. He is definitely an old man in need for sex, a closeted gay man who hides his true sexual orientation from his wife and children. Or maybe it's something else, despite the strange approach. But that's almost impossible, it's the first time I've seen him.

I smiled and looked at my watch. It was half past five. The two women I shared the table with left me. I thought I had sit in a gay bar, although the colourful crowd of guests did not confirm my assumption. Obviously, I was not only attracted to women, but also to men, old men. Interesting. I felt like Joe Buck, the midnight cowboy. I came to Geneva to entertain men. I had enough sense of humour, irony and self-irony.

I left the pub. The encounter with the strange man had unnerved me to the point where I could no longer sit still at the table and enjoy the evening sunlight reflecting off the surface of the lake. I forgot the slip of paper with the address. What I will do, I said to myself, but something pulled me back to the table where I was sitting. I went back. The paper was still on the table. I grabbed it, stuffed it into my pocket and left.

I was wandering the streets of the city, a restlessness overwhelmed me. I was getting more and more nervous. I pulled out a slip of paper from my pocket: 'Rue de Berne'. I am not far. Maybe it's not about sex. He was too upset. Maybe this would have been his first jump over the line to the male side, so he misjudged me thinking I was gay. Maybe the matter is more serious than I imagine. Why do I always think of sex first? Obsession? No, but a perfectly natural response, because I am a man who has never pushed his sexual need inside himself, but has satisfied it.

The curiosity aroused by the stranger in me drove me towards Rue de Berne. At half past seven, I was in front of house number twenty-one. Too soon. But you are crazy, I wondered. Have you turned gay? I was circling around building number twenty-one, my mind was blank, I wasn't thinking at all. All I knew was that I had to knock on the 'Private' door on the third floor. My hibernation was interrupted by the sound of a siren wailing on an ambulance driving on the Rue de Berne and stopping in front of number twenty-one. The paramedics entered the house I was about to enter at 8 am. They carried a stretcher. I thought of the man who was waiting for me. Did something happen to him? Did his heart fail? He couldn't bear the pressure of the burden he put on himself? Should I even enter, or should I forget the whole thing. I decided to head towards the Ibis Budget Hotel, where I had rented a room for a few days before moving into the Airbnb apartment I had rented for three months. Just as I was about to call a taxi, I heard a rumble outside house number twenty-one. Paramedics loaded a stretcher into the ambulance with an elderly woman lying on it. "So it wasn't him," I said to myself. I waited a few moments and then entered the five-storey house. I went towards the lift and got in, but left immediately and went up the stairs to the third floor. The lights turned on automatically when I entered the long corridor. I was looking for a door with the sign 'Private'. When I found the door where I was going, I stopped, took a deep breath and asked myself again, "What the hell am I doing?" This is my job; I said to myself and knocked on the door. It was exactly eight o'clock.

2

The light brown door slowly opened. The light from the corridor illuminated a small middle-aged black woman. In my judgement, she was Indian, Pakistani, or from Bangladesh. She looked at me with big dark eyes and asked me, in flawless English:

"Mr Mlinar?"

"That's me." I was immediately relieved to see the woman and glad that I would not be necessary to have sex with a man. But my sex-obsessed nature has already wanted to push them into further fantasising. But the lightning that struck me shook me so hard that it closed my windpipe. She knows who I am. How a foreigner in a foreign city knows the name of a stranger who arrived only yesterday.

Through a dark anteroom with three doors, left and right and straight ahead, she invited me straight into a large dark room. In the right-hand corner, by a curtained window was a free standing lamp with its glow pointing towards the ceiling. Along the wall to the right of the door was a small cupboard; on the opposite side was a large wooden table with six upholstered chairs. Along the wall where the door was, on the left side, was a large leather sofa, dark red. There was a man sitting there, who gave me a slip of paper with the address in the restaurant.

As soon as he saw me, he stood up and bowed. We didn't shake hands, he didn't say anything. He took his mobile phone out of his pocket and handed it wordlessly to the woman who opened the door. He put his right index finger to his mouth and gestured for me to do the same to hand over my phone to the woman. Without thinking, I took my phone out of my jacket pocket and gave it to her. Then the man took a piece of paper and wrote in English if I had some other electronic devices to hand over as well. I was just shaking my head.

Although I found this reception very strange, I agreed to the game they were playing with me. The woman put both phones in a clear plastic bag and took it into the anteroom through which we entered the apartment. The stranger and I waited wordlessly for her to return. She sat down next to a man on the part of the sofa closer to the door; and I sat down closer to the table. The man stood up, walked over to me and offered me his right hand:

"My name is Joseph McCormack. This is my wife Kamala. We both have PhDs in physics, she has a PhD in microbiology, and I have a PhD in nanotechnology. I know who you are, and I hope you will forgive us for being so direct and tactlessly, almost shamelessly dragging you to us."

"David Mlinar, freelance journalist. I am really surprised by everything that happened this afternoon and also surprised at myself for letting me be so easily seduced. We are journalists who are always ready to be attracted to the unknown, unexpected, possibly exclusive. I hope I'm not wrong."

"Not at all, Mr Mlinar," Joseph said again. "Let me tell you a few words about us, or maybe even before that, explain why and how we came to you. First of all, an apology for my behaviour in the bar, where you might have thought that I'm a fool who wants something from you."

"Actually, our interaction on the floor, when you handed me the slip of paper with the address where we are now, was really funny. What surprises me most is how you know where you will find me; as I just arrived in Geneva yesterday, and how do you even know who I am."

"Would you like something to drink? We have juice, water, and alcohol we don't have unfortunately."

"The water will be just fine." Kamala went to get water, Joseph continued:

"My wife and I are both members of a large international team of experts working under the auspices of CERN, but only for logistics and infrastructure reasons. Our research is not a part of CERN's activities. There, we also learned that you were coming to Geneva to do a longer report on the Nuclear Research Laboratory. We asked around about you and your work. We've scoured the web and gathered a lot of the information that made it easier for us to decide to contact you. Through you, we want to tell the world that humanity is in great danger and that all the conspiracy theories about the world's controllers behind the curtains are true. I must also mention our mutual friend, Lily Schweiger, Public Relations Officer at CERN, who has made all the necessary arrangements for your arrival and stay in Geneva, and from whom we got a lot of information about you. Yesterday, when you arrived at the hotel, we were already there. We wanted to contact you immediately, but unfortunately there was no opportunity to do so.

This morning, we were at the hotel very early and waiting for you. We followed you and waited for a good moment to contact you. When it looked like we were not going to make it, the table next to the one where you were sitting emptied. I was very upset because I'm a bad actor and a spy, but I had to come to you not to frighten you and drive you away. It turned out that I did a comedy that was entertaining all the people present there. I am glad that in all this awkwardness no one has noticed that I have handed over to you a slip of paper. So, again, my apologies if I have upset you in any way or put you in a bad mood."

"I must admit that I was quite surprised with your performance and your gesture when you dropped the invitation slip of paper with the address and the time into my hand. I had no explanation whatsoever behind it, except that it might be an indecent invitation. But despite that I was driven by journalistic curiosity, which is one of the attributes of our profession, especially in investigative journalism, which leads us into the unknown. I'm here now and available to satisfy my curiosity."

"The subject my wife and I want to talk to you about is very sensitive and dangerous. We think that it is life-threatening, but if we keep quiet about it, bad things will happen, things that are comparable to a large meteorite falling to Earth and destroying everything that lives on its surface. The intention we want to tell you about poses a risk for the existence of all mankind, a threat to the existence of free people, a threat to the existence of the world as we have known it for millennia. We want to give you, as brief as possible, a description of our problem and why we invited you, unwittingly forced you, to come to us. This is a very, very sensitive matter that very few people know about, because it is a project that could bring unimaginable breakthroughs to humanity in all areas, but which could become very dangerous and deadly in the hands of dangerous people, and that are certainly the masters of this world, and because of that we have to be very careful. Therefore, there must be no electronic devices at our meetings that could disclose our location or even enable eavesdropping of our conversations. We don't even use mobile phones. The phone you saw in my hand is empty, no circuit boards, and no battery. I only used it to show you to hand over your phone to my wife, who switched it off, put it in a plastic bag and took it to the safe in the next room. This apartment where we are meeting is not our apartment; it is just the space of the building manager, who is a good friend of ours."

"Interesting," I interrupted McCormack, taking off my jacket and putting it next to me. "I will do everything in my power to justify your trust and the effort you have put into this meeting." I turned into an ear.

"Maybe we should also agree on our communication and meetings, which should be kept to a minimum. We will agree on how to communicate. I suggest that every time we meet we agree on how we will communicate in the next meeting. Communication should not be done in a fixed, established way, but should be unique, first time, every time. Today we will use concrete words, but in the future we will try to avoid them. You must not write down or keep anything on paper or in any other form. Finally, I will hand you some documents related to this matter that we are going to discuss. I do not want to give this to you electronically because there is a greater risk of tracking and copying. These documents, which I will hand over to you, must be protected and guarded with the utmost secrecy and security. Of course, if you decide to take part in this project."

"No matter what you tell me, I have already decided to go with you to the end," I said, even though the fear alarm was going on inside me, making my head wedged and a tremendous press against my chest.

"So David, can I call you by your real name?"

"Of course, no problem."

"You can call me Joseph and my wife Kamala. We're from the United States of America. We studied physics together at Harvard, and then Kamala turned her attention to microbiology, and I to nanotechnology. After finishing our studies, we got married and worked together. We worked at NASA, and five years ago, we were invited to Geneva, where we joined a group of experts from different fields; most of us came from medicine and nanotechnology. Our task was to unify knowledge in nanotechnology, for the development and manufacture of nano-robots for use especially in medicine, so-called nano-medicine. It is about the use of materials and nano-scale devices for the diagnosis, prevention and treatment of disease. We are gathered in CERN, Geneva, where we are truly offered top-class conditions for carrying out our research work. As I have already told you, we are fully separated from their scientists and their work. From the start, I was bothered by the high level of secrecy around our research work, but I didn't want to worry about it. We were formally under the auspices of the World Health Organisation, but as I found out later, our work was abundantly funded by the world's biggest corporations.

Much has been done in this field, and in Geneva, we put it all on the table, selected the best, refined it and made a great step for humanity in fighting all kinds of diseases and in making life easier in general. Why nano, nano-devices, nano-medicine and so on. Because we are talking about an order of magnitude of ten to the power of minus nine metres; one billionth of a metre. To give you an idea, the size of atoms is between ten and a hundred pico-metres. A pico-metre is ten to the power of minus twelve of a metre. Human cells are ten to twenty micrometres in size, and a micrometre is one millionth of a metre, ten to the minus sixth power. So we're talking about the universe between the atom and the cell. These are devices that can remove the diseased cell, which can build the healthy cells needed for the affected tissue, or deliver a drug to the cells to ensure optimal absorption of the drugs without side effects. Kamala will tell you more.

Nanotechnology has long been a subject of interest for prestigious universities around the world, as well as for renowned corporations. For example, General Electric, Hewlett Packard, Synopsis, Northrop Grumman and Siemens. Our team includes scientists from all over the world, including Russia, China, Brazil, Australia, India and African countries. In fact, a crowd of scientists and experts has gathered to create a critical mass that could throw the planet off the course. And that's what happened. Nanotechnology is not only the technology of the future, it is also already the technology of the present, which in addition to medicine is also used in electrical engineering, engineering, construction, agriculture, even in space technology and in many other fields. Although nanotechnology is considered a modern technology and science, its origins go back a long way. The glaze used to line the ceramic vessels was made of nano-powder and nano-silver, and the food in these containers stayed fresh and usable for a longer period. The ship's floors were coated with a special copper emulsion to protect them from the fungi that were growing on the wood. Nano-products are nanometre-scale structures in dimensions that transform matter, energy and information using nanometre-scale components with well-defined molecular properties. Indeed, this technology has opened up whole new worlds, new universes in all areas of human creation. Unfortunately, nanotechnology is also already present in the military industry and most worryingly, what has actually already happened is that nanotechnology could control and manage people and their lives. And that is what we want to tell you. I hope I have not gone into too much detail about nanotechnology. I just wanted to describe this revolutionary new way of working to you in as simple and understandable a way as possible; a technology that has a dark side as well as a bright side. But more on that later, for now, I would like to give the floor to Kamala. Or maybe a question from you before that."

I was silent for a few moments, looking for the right question, but I didn't find it because there was a lot of information that already indicated which direction the conversation was going to take. I didn't want to interrupt their train of thought, so I replied:

"I have a lot of questions, but I think it's more important that you continue, because that way I'll probably get some answers. Maybe just who are these elite, who are the masters of the world, who act and influence the course of world events from behind the scenes? Who are these people?"

Joseph cleared his throat, folded his hands and said:

"I don't know, I don't know who these people are. All I know, and I am sure, is that they work through big corporations, banks, international organisations, formal and informal associations, and through politics, through national governments. And they are facilitated by various pacts, alliances, including the European Union, trade agreements and so on. I have not delved into the theories myself, but some things are clearer to me now, and what the real purpose of their existence is. I'm sure you'll find a lot more about these theories on the internet than I can tell you."

"Thank you, Joseph."

Then we sat in silence for a few moments and drank water. I have read and thought about the global elite, but there were so many contradictions, so many ambiguities, so much illogicality, that it seemed to me that these were just theories trying to simplify world events and their causes. Maybe that's why there are so many incredible stories around them to discourage people from believing in conspiracy theories.

Kamala began to speak in a very calm voice, the complete opposite of Joseph, whose speech was dramatic and, at times, apocalyptic, because the issue they wanted to present to me had the signs of a real cosmic revolution.

"I don't want to overburden you with too much information, with a long technical explanation of nano-medicine. Nano-medicine is the application of nanotechnology for medical purposes. This cutting-edge technology can be used to monitor, diagnose, treat and prevent disease. Today, we are so far away that each one of us could have hundreds of nano-devices, nanorobots, nano-sensors travelling around our bodies, detecting every anomaly in our cells, tissues, and organs. And then, we would feed the data into a computer at our personal doctor's office, which would alert him to what's happening in our body. Based on the data and computer projections, he would decide on a treatment, either by removing the diseased cells, which could be done by the nanorobots we already have in our body, by repairing and rebuilding the cells, or by injecting us with a new dose of these devices, loaded with drugs, which would deliver them directly to the diseased cells and ensure optimal dosing. But in practice, we have already passed this stage in the development of nano-robots in medicine, and we are now in the testing phase, where nano-robots do everything autonomously, without a doctor's authorisation. Before the doctor decides a form of therapy, nano-robots can already correct abnormalities and heal cells. These microscopic health workers, or doctors, if you prefer, get all the tools and materials they need to do their job successfully right inside the human body. Nano-machines, or molecular devices, could build new cells and new tissues at the level of molecules or even atoms. They mix and reconnect atoms to create the molecules they need. Nano-robots will also be involved in tissue engineering, helping to reproduce, repair or transform damaged cells, tissues and organs. Thus, they can very successfully replace conventional treatment with transplantation of diseased or damaged organs. Some prostheses will no longer be needed. For example, nanotechnology could be used to reconnect a severed blood vessel, restore a damaged lung, liver, kidney or any other organ. Nano-devices can connect the nervous system to the external computer to monitor and, if necessary, treat it. Parkinson's disease, or any disease of the nervous system, can be treated in this way.

We have developed high-performance and biodegradable nano-devices that can be injected into the human body. These devices also supply themselves with the bioenergy they need to function. They get their energy from glucose, which they extract from bio-fluids, which include human blood. They were first tested on animals and, contrary to expectations, the results were above average. It is enough to inject into the body one nano-robot or just a few. These nano-robots then build the next nano-robots by themselves, or reproduce themselves, and they carry out the tasks that are intended and programmed. The first experimental nano-robots have already been injected into volunteers. The nano-robots travel around the body and report any anomaly to an external computer, which is then used to correct the anomaly. For example, when cancer cells appear in the body, the nano-devices detect this and immediately send a message to the computer, which then processes the data and suggests more ways to cure the cells. These devices can be remotely reprogrammed, so they can be used for different operations. But as I said before, we are so far advanced in our research that these little robots would eliminate all anomalies automatically without the doctor's authorisation, which would be handled by computer algorithms developed for this purpose.

Can you imagine having first-aid with you at all times, carried around with you, working for you around the clock, seven days a week? In the evening, you lie down to rest and sleep until morning, but by the time the nano-robots detect a cell defect in an organ in your body, before you wake up in the morning, your little guardians have already made sure that the cell defect hasn't progressed to a tissue or whole organ defect. Your doctor has received a report on the night work of nano-robots. Can you imagine how this technology will relieve the burden on medicine, when there will be no more waiting for check-ups, no more hospital beds, no more huge numbers of surgical procedures, no more lengthy treatments, medicines and other pharmaceuticals. Can you imagine what this would mean for the underdeveloped world, where many people die of various diseases in addition to hunger? But here we run into another problem, which my husband will tell you more about.

In the initial phase, we envisaged that nano-robots would be injected only into the bodies of specific groups of people, for example the elderly, chronic patients, and then groups of people who are exposed to disease risks due to the specific nature of their occupation. For example, mining workers, industrial workers, soldiers, police officers. Anyone who is exposed to the negative effects of the environment on their body. Nanotechnology would also treat those who do not yet have these nano-devices inside them. In the next phase, all earthlings would carry nano-robots inside them to take care of healthy bodies. This could happen relatively quickly. The problem is not the production of nano-robots and their implementation, but the infrastructure and the organisation of the introduction of nano-robots into the body. And the ethical willingness of humanity to embrace such technology with full responsibility, so that its misuse can be minimised or even eliminated.

In short, we have made an incredible breakthrough in nanotechnology that will help humanity in medicine, pharmaceuticals, agriculture, environmental protection, construction, digitalisation, education, science, space exploration, practically in every field of human creation and exploration. This also raises questions about the Earth's population, birth control, which could also be controlled by nanotechnology instead of the current contraceptives. Could you imagine if you controlled your fertility through nano-robots, and when you decided to get pregnant, nanotechnology took care of it, opening the door to new life, or closing it if you didn't want to get pregnant? There are also questions about overpopulation, as well as ethical questions about human interference in the work of nature. Nanotechnology in agriculture can feed many more people than currently live on the planet, some estimates as high as one hundred billion. Space is also an issue, but again, nanotechnology can help solve it. There can be settled areas on Earth that are currently uninhabited and unsuitable for life, and of course we have the vast universe at our disposal. The first colonies on Mars are very close. In short, we can survive without war, without hunger, without poverty, if we really want to. But that's not for us scientists to decide, it's for the people behind us to decide, and for them to create the world according to their own plans. Joseph will tell you more about it. Is there anything you would like to ask, David? I'll be happy to answer you."

It took me a few moments to come back from the world Kamala had taken me to. It was really science-fiction for me and the not-very-powerful-computer in my head was too slow to process all the data and the information it had accepted. Nevertheless, I found a question for Kamala:

"Is it possible that the body does not accept injected nano-robots?"

"It is theoretically possible, but as I told you, these devices are made of biological substances that our bodies recognise and we already have in our bodies. We may encounter such a problem, but again, it can be solved with body-acceptable nano-bots injected for the sole purpose of correcting the anomaly."

"Thank you, Kamala."

I gave in to my hosts. The clock was rushing, but I was in no hurry. I had an appointment with Lily at 11 am. As long as they were ready to talk, I didn't want to disturb them. I was completely captivated by their story. Joseph continued.

3

"Dear David, we have now come to the moment when we must tell you why we kidnapped you in the first place and dragged you to us. Our intention was not to lecture you on nanotechnology, on nano-medicine, on nanorobots, on nano-devices, on all these nano-stuff you probably haven't heard much about before. Am I wrong, David?"

"No, Joseph, you are not mistaken. I have heard and read a little about nanotechnology, but only in passing. I have never had such an insight. Fantastic."

"If you like, we can conclude at this point, because from here on there is no longer a renaissance for humanity, but it's Armageddon. You can reject us, or perhaps betray us. It's your free will."

"No way, Joseph."

"Do you want me to continue?"

"Absolutely. That is why I am here. As a concerned Earthling and as an investigative journalist, I want to hear what you have to say." Adrenaline flooded me, along with a hard-to-describe uneasy feeling that crawled over me and overwhelmed me, like a low fog over the sea. Joseph continued:

"As my wife has already said, we are already technologically ready to implement this technology in society, both in medicine and in other areas. Of course, this would not happen overnight, but over several years. I am sure it will be sooner than ten years. But to take this revolutionary step in the use of nanotechnology, especially in medicine, we Earthlings need to be ethically mature enough. Above all, politics, or rather, the people who run our planet, should be morally robust so that they do not succumb to the various temptations and pitfalls that have accompanied humanity since Eve and Adam. There should be a revolution of spirit, a revolution of values, above all, a revolution of humanity. For those who hold most of the capital in this world, for those who set governments and presidents, for those who decide war and peace, life and death; for those who exploit our labour and as soon as they can no longer earn with us, we become useless eaters for them, for them, nanotechnology is a different challenge than for humanity. For them, the poor, the hungry, the sick, the disabled, the different, and the elderly are just a burden. They do not see the benefit in not having hungry people in the world, not having sick people, not having people live for a hundred, a hundred and twenty years or more. For them, the only people who matter are the people they can exploit. But when their value drops, when they are no longer a hundred percent at their work, when they grow old, they are just a burden, an insect, a scum. Owners of the means of production need less and less live labour. It is being replaced by autonomous robots which need low-maintenance, unlike humans. Robots can also replace soldiers or police officers. All lower-skilled jobs can be done by robots. The masters of the world will only need loyal, highly qualified individuals to keep the world in order according to their needs and plans. Their loyalty will be richly rewarded by their hosts. And it is precisely because of these people, who combine all the negative attributes of greed, power-hunger, egoism, hostility, bloodthirstiness, that the world as we know it is doomed to collapse.

I have never been a fan of conspiracy theories. I have never been interested in the Freemasons, the Illuminati, the Bilderbergers, the various clubs and associations that run the world from the depths of hell. For me, it was all a fairy tale to pass the time. I did not have the time to deal with such matters, nor the interest. I never imagined that the world is not as we know it. The world is a chessboard on which the masters play chess with us, who are the chess pieces. For them, everything is a game; wars, disease, famine, lack of drinking water, poverty. Whatever the human mind has created throughout history to save lives, to make life easier, the masters have used to destroy lives. Every weapon from the bow to the atomic bomb, from generals to computers that successfully replace the human brain, have all been used to dominate and control the world. Scientists are supposed to be working for the good of humanity, but this is not the case. Scientists are also just people tempted by demons. But Kamala and I decided to tell *Urbi et Orbi* about the conspiracy in which we were also unwitting participants. That's why we turned to you. I apologise for the long introduction. This address of mine is not only dictated by the brain, but by something more, perhaps by the spirit itself, which in this case, thank God, is stronger.

About a month ago, all of us nano-scientists were at the project leader's board. When the meeting was over, the manager asked me if I could stay a little longer to discuss a matter that had nothing to do with our work. Before we even started talking, he was called to one department. He asked me to wait a few minutes until he returned. I was left alone in the meeting room. I sat for a while and then I started walking around the hall. When I passed by the computer on the desk where the manager was sitting, I subconsciously looked at the screen. I read, 'Strictly confidential!' My curiosity compelled me to read on. What I have read has astonished me. I had a small data storage device in my pocket, so I plugged it into the computer and copied the file onto it without a second thought. It was like a movie. As I dropped the USB key back into my jacket pocket and walked a little away from the table, the manager returned. We talked for a few minutes, then I told him I wasn't feeling well and that I was going home. As soon as I got home, I sat down at the computer and started reading."

4

Joseph continued:

"What I read was so astonishing and shocking that it took me a long time to even comprehend what I had read. For me, it was like the death sentence of the innocent, the reversal of the poles, the fall of Olympus, the extinction of life on Earth. It was the realisation that all the life you had lived was in vain, worked in vain, that you had lived in a lie, in another world. All my life, all my knowledge, all my work collapsed into nothing that day.

A critical mass of scientists has gathered in CERN to help humanity, but our knowledge, work and efforts will be used by the masters of our lives to remake the world according to their satanic plans. Nano-robots will be used primarily to control and manipulate people, enslave them, even kill them. My wife and I turned to you because we thought that you, the journalists, might be the only hope to prevent this. We did not dare to talk about this with our colleagues because we do not know how much they are involved in this conspiracy. So all this immense effort, tens, hundreds, thousands, millions of hours of work and research, all this knowledge, has been devoted solely to the goal of managing the people. The nano-robots we will carry in our bodies will be designed to control us. They will monitor our movements, our work, and our state of health, our thoughts, and our mind. If they deem us useful, they will use the nano-robots to help us recover in case of illness; otherwise they will shut us down or kill us. Their plan is very meticulous and does not allow for any mistakes or obstacles.

In the next few years, an artificially created virus will be released from the laboratory to the surface of the Earth, affecting the human respiratory system. It will spread very quickly because it will be transmitted by droplets and aerosols, which means that an infected person will pass it on to another person by exhaling air from his lungs or by sneezing and sniffling. It will be a very persistent virus that will survive in all conditions. Neither extreme heat nor extreme cold will be able to stop it. Then they will very quickly invent a vaccine against this virus, which was in fact created along with the virus. But this vaccine will only be a stepping stone on the road to human subjugation. The vaccine will prove unreliable as new and newer versions of the virus, more and more deadly, are released into the human population, increasing panic and fear. It will be the weak, the elderly, and the sick – people who are a burden to the masters of the world – who will die. Then they will start to tighten the situation. They will actually unleash a deadly virus on people. They will also make a vaccine to stop the virus very soon. Anyone who refuses to be vaccinated could have severe respiratory problems and the death rate among infected people will certainly be very high. Rulers will start persecuting those who refuse to be vaccinated on the pretext that they want to protect the world's population. They will lose their jobs, they will be banned from moving around, their property will be legally seized, their medical treatment will be made more difficult, and they will lose all the human rights that we have known, at least on paper, until now. They will become leprous outcasts, killed not only by disease, but also by rabid vaccinated people because, despite the antibodies they will receive from the vaccine, they will be convinced that they are at risk from those who will refuse the vaccine. This will be done by carefully planned propaganda, thus encouraging and tolerating lynching. With the virus vaccine, they will release into our bodies nano-robots that will truly eliminate a deadly virus while taking over control over our bodies, and later over our minds. As I have learned from the documents I have looked at, part of the team of scientists has already developed an algorithm for nano-robots to control and influence the human mind with specific commands. And as the culmination of everything, the mind control of the individual. Can you imagine being told from the outside how to think and act, so that your every autonomous thought is monitored. We will become robots. As long as we are useful to the rulers, they will keep us in good shape. When they no longer need us, or if some individuals might mentally and spiritually resist subjugation, they will kill us with cancer or some other deadly disease via occupying nano-robots. They will simply switch us off, shut us down.

    My wife and I wonder whether it is possible to stop this madness, this cataclysm of humanity. I am afraid that if the masters happened to find out that the information had leaked outside their bubble, they would certainly kill us. Therefore, we must be cautious all the time. David, give me your opinion on what I have just told you?"

What I heard completely paralysed me. I thought I was dreaming; that I was drugged, that I was in another world and strange beings from other planets were experimenting on me. I was so shocked that I could hardly raise my hand and gestured that I needed some time to collect myself. After a few moments of silence, I uttered:

"I am shocked. I still hope that maybe it is not as apocalyptic as you said. I do not know how to even define what you have told me. As a conspiracy theory, as a science fiction story, or as fact. Forgive my nonsense. It's so crazy that if I wrote an article about it, nobody would believe me. I don't know if anyone would even want to publish something like that."

"Don't you believe me, David?" asked Joseph.

"I believe you, but my brain simply rejects the theory."

"Everything is as I read it. You will see for yourself. I destroyed the USB stick where I had stored the incriminating documents' file. You now have the only copy printed on these sheets, which I am now handing to you. What will you do with it, I don't know. Into your hands, to a perfect stranger, we give our lives and the future of the planet. I hope we haven't made the mistake of a lifetime, because with the best will in the world, we don't know who we can trust."

"You are completely safe with me. But if that is the case, then the moment I publish this, my life will be worth less than a grain of sand in the desert. I cannot think soberly at the moment. There is so much fantastic information in my head that I can't process it so quickly. I will take the documents, read them carefully and consider what options we have. Where can I reach you if I have any questions?"

"Here is the key to the mailbox in this house that nobody uses. Leave a message inside and you will find the reply, or messages from our side. Take your time. How long will you stay in Geneva?"

"I had planned for three months, but considering these new circumstances, I'll probably leave sooner."

"We will have time to think carefully about our next steps, or to resign ourselves to a destiny designed by the masters of the world."

"I hope you don't mind, I'll leave now."

"No way, David. Go with God."

I went out at night. I wasn't interested in what hour it was. I wandered aimlessly through the illuminated streets of a city that had suddenly become a city of terror, a city demolishing my mind, a city of the apocalypse that was about to happen. I began to ponder what I had heard. It all made sense to me in theory, but I couldn't accept that it would actually happen. Not today. Are we humans in this world really just puppets, extras, experimental animals? Are there really dark forces that control the world, life and death? Is it really possible that our freedom is just an illusion, just a false belief that we are masters of our bodies and minds? Is it true that what is happening in the world is just a show, just a reality show? Or is the world just a zoo, a laboratory, and we humans are the animals that are being watched and inhuman experiments are being done on them. There was no way that my untamed freethinking could accept such considerations. No, no and no. Surely Joseph must have missed something, misunderstood. As an investigative journalist who sought and researched facts and causes, who always worked on the basis of reason and intellect, I did not accept the various conspiracy theories about the Illuminati, about Luciferian groups, about Freemasons, about lizards, about aliens, about the devil being omnipresent in the world. Now these theories are about to become reality. With my common sense, I cannot accept that. I didn't want to think, just walk, and walk. I don't know what time it was when I got to the hotel. I threw myself into the bed and fell asleep instantly, dressed in the clothes I came in and wearing my shoes as if the invisible lord of the world had hit me over the head with a club.

5

In the distance, I heard a phone buzzing. I looked at the watch, half past twelve. Eleven o'clock, CERN, fuck. Lily called me. We agreed to have lunch at one o'clock and talk afterwards. Where I am? Who am I? I undressed and ran to the shower. I don't know how long it rained on me before I actually woke up. I remembered Joseph and Kamala; I remembered what they had told me.

"I'll think about that later, now it's CERN's turn," I said to myself and let the tiny drops massage my body for a while. I convinced myself not to think about yesterday, but every now and then, an alarm would go on, alerting me to tectonic shifts that had occurred the previous day and that my inner senses had detected. Illusions, auditory hallucinations, apparitions, phantoms?

Lily was a very nice brunette in her late thirties and if it hadn't been for that incomprehensible and catastrophic cloud over my head, I would have spent so much time trying to get into her knickers. I didn't want sex, I didn't want anything. I left CERN in the late afternoon and took a taxi to the hotel. I lay down on my bed and started reading the documents that Mr and Mrs McCormack had given me.

I read until three in the morning. Then I spent the next day thinking about what I had read. I was free, with no commitments. After that night, and especially after what I had read, I would not have been prepared to do anything because I was clinically dead. I needed reanimation. After three hours of staring at the ceiling, with my senses switched off, I regained consciousness enough to go into the bathroom and let a waterfall from the shower of hot, cold water. I felt nothing for a while. When the disoriented mind and, consequently, the body woke up, the water was too hot. I stood in the shower for a while until I felt myself coming back to life. After breakfast, I moved into my rented flat, and then I lay down in bed and started to drag out what I had heard from the McCormacks and what I had read.

The document I read talked about reducing the number of people on Earth and robotising and reprogramming those that remain. An incredibly detailed plan with all the elements that a good document of this kind requires. A description of the status quo and then the course of the gradual depopulation of the world and the enslavement of those who will be left alive, with a specific goal in mind. Five hundred million inhabitants on Earth is the goal within thirty years at the latest. More than seven billion people will be wiped out, destroyed, killed. Seven billion unnecessary eaters, seven billion removals, seven billion murders with impunity. What sick minds, what people are behind this terrible plan? Has God abandoned us to the devil?

Nowhere was it possible to read who the people behind this plan are. They will not kill people with armies and sophisticated weapons, but with viruses twenty to three hundred nanometres in size. With the intermediate vaccines, they will essentially be doing multi-level selection of humans until they reach the planned number of Earthlings. First they will kill the weakest, the sick children and adults, the disabled, the handicapped, the elderly. Then they will use a series of new viruses to select those who remain and control births. They will get rid of the Third World poor in particular. The chosen ones will be rescued and at the same time enslaved by the nano-bots they will receive via a vaccine that will save them from the deadly virus. The slaves chosen will be mainly highly skilled individuals and their family members, who will serve the interests of the elite and will be able to rule the world smoothly, without wars, without hunger and poverty, without disease. They will not need a large army, nor a large police force. There will be only one country, one government in the world. All low-and medium-skilled jobs will be done by robots, transport will be provided by automated vehicles and planes, which will be collective, part of public transport. There will be no private transport, except for the elite. Private property will also be gone. Slaves will spend their holidays in nearby complexes built for them, with man-made seas, islands, deserts, glaciers, forests, even mountains. The real places, where once throngs of tourists flocked, will remain accessible only to the elite and the first rank of their slaves. Robots will produce the goods slaves need to live. There will be no more consumer society as we know it. There will be no more money in physical form. People will work most of the time and be happy because they will have their illusory happiness instilled in them by nano-robots. They will receive family planning from nano-family counsellors. Their lives will be controlled by nano-controllers, working at the behest of larger computer systems controlled by the world's elite. Everything is well planned and will be carefully controlled. There will be no more people; there will be no more God.

Am I dreaming? Am I crazy? Am I drugged? Am I living in a parallel world? I needed air, fresh air. I went out and wandered around the city. I drank a few beers and went back to my flat, a bit tipsy, and drank another cognac. I don't remember when I fell asleep. The next day I woke up very early. I spent the day in CERN, where I met Kamala. She looked at me blankly, but we didn't speak. I put as much effort into the work I came to Geneva to do as it took to get it done.

Without excess, without me, without my soul. Lily and I have grown closer. I needed her; I needed sex to break the stream of thoughts running through my head. The end of the world was approaching and I knew about it, but I had no idea what to do. How do I tell the planet that it is about to collapse? The moment I announce, anywhere in the world, that there is a cosmic genocide in the making, my life will not be worth a pigeon's droppings. They will kill me the very next day, and they will kill everyone who was, in any way, connected to me. The caravan will go on.

I needed to use the time I would spend in Switzerland to think carefully about what to do, because I knew I had to do something, I couldn't live with it anymore. I was not afraid for my life, I was afraid for the lives of innocent people who have no idea what the guardians of the planet are up to. I was afraid of the fear that would reign in the world. Nothing will ever be the same again. Even Robin Hood couldn't save us. Where were Batman and Superman then, when we needed them? Where was Chuck Norris? Where were the various messiahs and prophets, the demigods, the deities? Where was God?

6

I forgot about the arrangement with McCormacks. Fourteen days after we met, I had not looked in the letterbox at 21 Rue de Berne. I rushed out of CERN to the place where my previous life ended and a new life began, long torture, disfigure, giving up, and dying slowly. I even thought of suicide, which I could not accept and I was against self-killing, self-destruction. Bang and I'm gone, a stone around my neck in the lake, a car into a wall, alcohol and pills, blood and water. No, I cannot kill myself. Let them kill me, I will not kill myself. In the mailbox was a small slip of paper that read 4-6-8. I quickly decoded the message. The 6th of April at 8. I missed two days. I wondered whether I should leave a message. I decided not to leave any message. They will know that I was here because I took their message with me.

The next day the slip read XX-X. At first, I thought they were proposing to meet on the 20th, but it seemed too far away. The next day I knocked on the door at 8 pm. I waited a few moments. I knocked again. Joseph opened the door for me. Without a word, we entered the apartment and sat down in the same way as the first time.

"Hello David. How are you?"

"Hello Joseph. I don't know if I am. I don't think so, so I am not. I still cannot accept all that has accumulated in my head. I cannot accept that the world and the life I have known and lived until now will be no more. Terrible; it is as if I had begun to die in the worst agony. I don't know what to say to you. I do not condemn you for entrusting me with this terrible plan to destroy humanity, but I would have been better if I had not known this devil's plan. Maybe you didn't choose me, maybe I was chosen by God or the devil. Joseph, I don't feel well. I realise there is no turning back."

"I'm so sorry I ruined your life."

"No Joseph. Maybe that's better. I can prepare for the end of the world and finally make peace with myself and the universe. I might even save the whole world," I joked, smiling a very sour smile.

"Maybe so," Joseph continued. "That's exactly why I wanted to meet you. Unfortunately Kamala could not make it today. What I am about to tell you is perhaps a glimmer of hope for all of us, for humanity, for the planet. I didn't tell you last time that we have also created nano-robots, which are designed to quickly destroy nano-bots that have already been injected into the body. We made them to be used in case of any malfunction, software or technological, on the devices in the body. A few days ago, we completed this chapter and now we have an army of nano-robots that might enter the body afterwards. What do you think about this, David?"

"How will you do it? Can you make these nano-robots outside CERN? Can you do it on your own without help from others? How do you plan to inject them into people out of control?"

"Kamala and I have been thinking about this too. We won't be able to save the world, but we can stand up to the global elite and put some sand between their wheels. Kamala and I will be returning to the United States within a few days, up to a maximum of fourteen. We will continue our work in NASA, where we were before this Swiss adventure. We are convinced that we can make nano-robots there that can be used in a guerrilla war against the conspiracy in which we have unwittingly participated. We don't have a detailed plan on how to do it yet, but I'm sure it's doable."

"How are you going to convince people to take these anti-robots into their bodies? This is practically impossible."

"I know it sounds utopian, but it is a possibility, and we will do everything we can to ensure that as many people as possible receive these anti-robots, as you call them. I would also ask you to help us. We can also invite friends we trust into this guerrilla war. We know a few people we can trust. I hope you and your friends will join us."

"I need to think about this carefully. Should a few people stand up to the people who rule the world? It sounds hopeless and suicidal."

"What is there left for us, dear David?"

I was silent for a few moments; then I shot out: "I'm in." of course I was in, because I had no other options. Rebellion was the only option that still made life worth living.

"I'm glad you're with us. Organising our group and communicating between us will require a lot of care, ingenuity and money. Kamala and I have plenty of money spared. She is from a very wealthy family, so we will make sure we can operate smoothly."

"When will you have the first anti-robots?"

"We hope very soon. We will communicate directly. You will be visiting us in America; of course we will pay all the costs. We will meet for the first time in Whistler, British Columbia, on the west coast of Canada. We have a holiday home there and you can fly to Vancouver and then rent a car and drive to us in two hours. Here, on this slip of paper, you have the address and a phone number in Canada, but you should only use it in an emergency. I'm also handing you fifty thousand dollars in cash to get you started, and a credit card that you can use. The daily limit is ten thousand dollars, which can be released."

"Do you really trust me that much?"

"Of course we trust you. What have we got to lose? Some money. Otherwise, it's your money. As a successful investigative journalist, we're giving you seven hundred thousand dollars for your work. Here is a document confirming that the fund Kamala and I manage has donated this money to you. To this end, we have opened an account here in Switzerland, which you are now managing."

Shock after shock. Everything was happening fast, too fast. I had hardly followed. My thinking was interrupted by Joseph:

"When can you come to Whistler?"

"In the second half of June, for sure. I'll be in Geneva for a while, probably until mid-May. Then I'll go to Melbourne, where I have a good friend I can trust with this story."

"Great, then Kamala and I are expecting you on the 25th of June."

"I will come on the 25th of June."

"Until then, we will not communicate with each other. In case you need to communicate, please call the number on the slip. Leave a message on the answering machine that contains nothing that could disclose us."

"OK. I have one question for you. Even though we are going into revolt against the masters, am I trying to find a channel to disperse information about the conspiracy? I don't think it would make sense to irritate them, because then they would be more alert and we and our work could be at risk. But I would also like to hear your opinion."

"You have come to the right conclusion. No information should be shared and we must be very careful because the slightest mistake can lead to loss of life. And this, if you need to call our number in Canada, please do so from a neutral phone, preferably a public payphone."

"Absolutely. Did you have anything else to say?"

"No. I think we've agreed on everything we need to do. My wife and I trust you completely, but be careful about who you share information with."

"You can be completely worry-free. Give my regards to Kamala."

"Thank you very much."

"Good luck."

We shook hands and repeated the date, the 25th of June, Whistler, British Columbia in Canada.

When I left, I had seven hundred fifty thousand dollars in my head. Do they really have that much trust in me, or are they setting a trap for me? I don't know why, I wondered. I decided to move on. If it stinks, I'll back off.

7

I was looking forward to staying in Geneva for spring before I arrived, but now I want to leave as soon as possible. But I had to do the job I came to do. I focused on it, so I spent a lot of time in CERN. I sent reports before the deadline to the subscriber. I spent many evenings and nights with Lily. Sometimes she stayed in my apartment, or I stayed in hers. I needed her because I felt lonely and abandoned. Our relationship was completely free. We both knew that we had no future together, so we lived for the moments we spent with each other. We had a nice time.

But every moment I had to myself, my mind was flooded with nano-robots. I got to know them well. I had read everything I could get on the internet about them. I had also read about the Illuminati, the Freemasons, the Jesuits, the Bilderbergers, various secret societies, everything written by conspiracy theorists. Although I still found it very difficult to accept, intellectually, the various theories about the visible and the invisible world, now, when I find myself in the middle of a global conspiracy, I see things and events in the world differently. Globalisation has happened to extend the influence and subordination of large companies, corporations, societies, to acquire new markets on a carrot-and-stick basis and ensuring continuous pressure on individual governments. And the International Monetary Fund, together with the World Bank, has designed financial policy and forced individual countries into debt. If any country has not succumbed to globalist pressure, it has become Venezuela, or democracy has been exported to it by military force. I've seen connections where I hadn't seen them before.

I was going to tell Brian everything. He needed to hear this, so I planned to travel to Melbourne immediately after I finished my work at CERN. Brian and I had been friends for many years. I could trust him. He was a journalist like me. We had been together in Afghanistan, Bolivia, North Africa and Antarctica. I was sure that he was not under the patronage of any intelligence service, so I could trust him completely. I was planning to leave Geneva at the end of May. First, I was planning to go home for a few days, then travel to Australia, and from there to Canada.

Even though I hadn't planned to see the McCormacks again, I would occasionally turn into Rue de Berne and look in the letterbox. When fourteen days had passed since my last meeting with Joseph, I spontaneously decided to go one last time to check the letterbox beside that they will or have already travelled back to the United States. There was a slip in the mailbox that said only twenty-six. I understood the message, the meeting on the twenty-sixth. The time is certainly the same as before, 8 pm. I thought, immediately; in fact, I was sure that they had something very urgent to tell me because they should have left already. This time, I was welcomed by both of them. Joseph was very agitated and Kamala's Eastern calm had left her.

"Sorry to call you again, David," Joseph began. "Unfortunately, something happened that scared us very much. The project leader died suddenly. We have been told that he did not survive the heart attack he suffered three days ago. Under normal circumstances, I would accept this as something that can happen to anyone. This time, I am not sure he died of cardiac arrest. I accept that I may be wrong and have unnecessarily upset you, but it is better to be cautious. Maybe they removed him after the project was finished because they no longer needed him, or maybe they found something incriminating about him and had to eliminate him. When I copied the file from the manager's computer, I didn't think about the surveillance cameras recording the action in the hall. It is possible that they saw me when I was switching on the computer. But if that were true, I would surely be dead by now. Or it is possible that they have set a trap for me and Kamala and they are monitoring me, and now they know that we are meeting with you. Anything is possible. If the latter is true, then that's the end of us. I am very sorry that we put your life in danger."

"Joseph, don't look at it so blackly. Of course, what you have said is possible, but I doubt that it is. If they really knew that you had looked into the leader's computer and copied its contents, you would have been killed the next moment, without a second thought, with Kamala next to you. They would not wait for you to spread this information around. Even if you were allowed to meet me, which I very much doubt, we would have been murdered together. I'm sure they wouldn't give you a millionth of a second to spread that information. From this I conclude, my dear Joseph, that they do not know about us. I not only think so,

I am convinced of it. Did your leader die naturally, or whether they provoked a heart attack, or otherwise killed him, will remain unexplained. We cannot rule out the possibility that he was killed. If he was really murdered, it was because he was no longer needed by them."

Kamala answered:

"I told him the same thing, but this tragedy scared him so much that he stopped thinking soberly, and he pulled me into this conspiracy theory. You are right when you say that if they knew about us they would remove us immediately. But let's definitely take this as a warning and a reminder to be even more careful together."

Joseph was silent for a few moments. After a while, he spoke:

"I agree with you and I hope so. In view of the seriousness of the event and as an extra precaution, I would suggest that we do not meet at our house in Whistler. Do you play golf, David?"

"I'm not a keen golfer, and I'm not a complete beginner either."

"Excellent. Then we will meet at the restaurant on the golf course. The address is written on the slip."

I looked at the slip of paper and it said:

"Nicklaus North GC, IX-XI. Table XIX, XXX." Apparently XXX meant the 30th instead of the 26th, and IX-XI between the 9th and 11th hours. Certainly in Whistler, because it said nothing else. Table XIX told me nothing. But my embarrassment was solved by Joseph:

"Table Nineteen is the name of the restaurant on the golf course."

"Thank you."

Then we said goodbye. I went to my Geneva apartment and thought about what the McCormacks had told me. Once again, I had come to the conclusion that we were not threatened by the dark forces of the world at that moment. That was why we had to continue our resistance, which was the only hope of stopping or at least slowing down the implementation of the infernal plan. This meeting with Joseph and Kamala had a positive effect on me and gave me a new amount of energy and will to fight the invisible enemy, who would sooner or later launch an offensive.

8

I left Geneva on the 28th of May. I had planned to fly to Melbourne on the 5th of June. I stayed at my mum's house for a week, where I met Beti. I missed her. All these events that happened in Switzerland shook me up and all I wanted at that moment was to meet my mother and Beti. I wanted her. I wondered if it was too selfish to rush at her and squeeze her to me. Isn't that too hypocritical, after I was with Lily for two months, enjoying sexual fantasies and taking advantage of each other? Is it fair to mess with poor Beti head even more, to take advantage of her and then go away again? But I needed Betty, not her body.

I have not come to any real conclusion about what to do with the information about the planetary conspiracy. I needed to brainstorm it with Brian, David Luiz, Wang Shu and Marghrete. I trusted them. I had a long journey ahead of me: Australia, Canada, Brazil, Hong Kong, and Denmark…Where else would the path lead me to find the solutions for the world? What could we do? Could we resist the evil that threatens us? What were our options, if any? Questions, questions, questions. Lots of unanswered questions. I didn't want to give up; it was the only option I had left, despite the very bad prognosis for the future. I thought to myself, *if I have to die sooner than the stars told me, I would die fighting. I would not give up.* Together with my friends I was going to organise a worldwide guerrilla to resist the invaders. Friends have friends. The numerousness had given us hope. But we had to be careful.

I arrived home late in the evening. I came unannounced. Mum was having a party. She was already a bit intoxicated. I didn't want to spoil her fun, so I went straight to my room. The next morning, she was waiting for me in the kitchen.

"Why didn't you tell me you were coming? I wouldn't have had any party."

"I wanted to surprise you," I lied to her. I didn't want to tell her that I had no intention of calling, as I always did, because I expected her to be waiting for me at home.

"I could prepare you dinner and we could talk."

"We're talking."

"What's wrong with you? Something is bothering you?"

I felt like telling her everything, I trusted her, but that might have been signing my own death warrant. Or so I thought at the time.

"I'm tired. I'll be home for a few days to rest and then I'll be on my way again."

"Where are you going this time?"

"To Australia, to Brian. Remember when he was with me in Slovenia two years ago?"

"Of course I remember him, the real Crocodile Dundee. A little bit rough, but a real man. We emptied quite a few bottles of wine together. Say hello to him and tell him I haven't forgotten his promise to visit us again this year."

"Maybe he will come. We have to do something together, and then there is a real chance that he will come to Slovenia."

"Now, just tell me what's bothering you. I am your mother and I can see in your face that you are not OK."

I was looking for a suitable lie, I had to lie.

"Just before I left home, my host in CERN died suddenly. We became true friends, so I was devastated by his death."

"I understand you, my son. But death is a part of this fucking life. We will all die one day."

"What would you do if you knew that you would die next year, for example?"

"I wouldn't do anything. All my life I have lived as if I will live to be a hundred years old or die next year. I wouldn't change anything in my life."

"I understand. What if, for example, scientists predicted that in two years' time a large meteorite would hit the Earth, destroying all living things, all life?"

"Is that what they told you in CERN, that a big meteorite is coming?"

"No, I'm just asking because I've been thinking a lot about the death that so suddenly interrupted the link with my friend in Geneva."

"As I said, I wouldn't change anything. I would live as before. But it would be very distressing to see desperate people going mad, throwing themselves out of windows from the twentieth floor, getting drunk, drugging, and killing. There will be chaos. It's better not to know what's coming."

"It's better not to know what's coming," the phrase echoed in my head. The days when I was at home were spent with Beti or my mother. I asked Beti the same question as my mother. But her reaction was completely different from

Mum's. She would be in the group of people my mother described, the suicidal. She would probably go mad. I didn't poke them with these questions anymore. I tried to act as normal as possible and put on my face a mask of indifference. I didn't think I managed to convince either of them. My mother knew me well, and so did Beti. Before I left, my mother told me:

"Take care, my boy."

And Beti was crying, inconsolably, as if we would never see each other again. What to do with her, I wondered. I didn't want to leave her because I needed her. She was what I was consciously afraid of, but subconsciously I wanted her.

I took the taste of her lips with me to Australia.

9

As we were flying over the Pacific, I suddenly wished that the plane would crash and thus save me from an ominous future. My subconscious was a constant reminder that I will never have peace again. I have to solve this rationally if I am not going to go mad. Spirituality? I made fun of it, well, not exactly made fun of it; I didn't take it as something that could be part of human life in an advanced world. It seemed to me more like some deception of the mind. In fact, I never thought about it. What is spirituality? Is it a deliberate disregard of the mind, to go with the flow and what will be, it will be.

I rested my head on the glass of the cabin window and stared out into the night. I could feel the vibrations of the plane and listen to the hum of its engines. I didn't think about anything, nothing was in my head. I was just breathing, barely perceptibly. I only breathed in so much air, as far as necessary. I was not awake, but I was not asleep, or so it seemed to me. I wasn't there; I wasn't sitting in the seat of the plane that flew from Dubai to Melbourne. I found myself in a calming whiteness that completely overwhelmed me. I wanted to stay in it. I was called out by a stewardess who wanted to know if I needed anything.

Brian was waiting for me at the Melbourne airport. In the car on the way from the airport to his home, I told him everything.

"What do you mean, Brian?"

"David, I'm not surprised at all. The only thing that surprises me is that this has already started to happen. I have never bothered you with my thoughts and what I have followed and know about the various conspiracy theories. But it all made sense, it was all connected, even if at first glance it seems like a fairy tale born in the minds of crazy people."

"How to deal with that?"

"We can try media publications. But we will achieve nothing. There are many different stories circulating on the web, some true, some fictional. Intelligence services make sure that fake news covers up real information.

Dozens of different messages are released to the public, some of them authentic, but difficult to identify. If tomorrow, we knock on the door of my friend who is editor-in-chief of The Australian and tell him this story, he will throw us out of his office. Not because he wouldn't believe us, but because he fears for his safety. No one is safe from the scavengers behind it all. Do you remember the death of Polish President Kaczynski? He was probably killed because he resented the global mafia. According to some information, shortly before his death, he agreed to assist Asian countries in their demands for the return of the United States' off-balance debt, which was made through the decades of the twentieth century, when gold was taken from the East by the Western countries, and in return, the US Federal Reserve issued off-balance bonds. But after the debentures expired, America evaded paying them and continues to evade the solution of this problem. Far East countries looked for help in Europe and found it at Kaczynski. Two days after his consent, he died. Coincidence?"

"What do you suggest then, that I just swallow all this crap and watch the world collapse before my eyes? Something needs to be done."

"I absolutely agree. But this requires a strategy for getting the word out. We must also take care of our own safety, because if we are killed, no one will benefit except those who decide our fate."

"One problem is how to inform the public. The second problem is how to vaccinate people with the vaccine that Joseph and his wife will produce. Before we parted in Geneva, they told me that they would be able to build nano-robots in America that would be deaf to the commands sent by the masters' computers and would be tasked with destroying their nano-robots. We should vaccinate as many individuals in the world as possible with these anti-robots to ensure a critical mass of people are not enslaved."

"This will be an even bigger problem than the launch of the conspiracy information. I don't know how you are going to convince people to accept a vaccine into their bodies that has not been approved by the World Health Organisation, by the governments, or by the official medical profession. Illegal vaccination would be immediately disclosed, because information would surely be leaked from the crowd of people who might have been vaccinated. We would be slaughtered in an instant."

"We will discuss this further. That is why I flew to you. Let's postpone this until tomorrow. Today I have had enough of this nano-disaster. I need rest and a long sleep. I forgot to tell you that I won't be staying with you, but in a hotel near you. I think it is better that way."

"Right, although Karen and I have prepared a room for you, which you've always used. Come to dinner tonight. Karen is a very good cook. At eight."

"OK."

I got off at the hotel near Brian's flat. Every time I visited him, he had a different woman. The previous one was Thelma, now Karen. He was a hunter, just like me, but he lived with them. I lived with my mother.

When I got to my room, I undressed and went to take a shower. Before that, I phoned Beti and my mum and told them that I had arrived safely in Melbourne. Then I drank a glass of whisky. I fell asleep in an armchair, woke up in bed at 6 pm. I was hungry, but I had to wait until eight. I started to reflect on our conversation on the way to the town from the airport. Brian told me what I already knew. It would be difficult. But we would have to do something. Step by step. I definitely needed to talk to David Luiz, Wang Shu and Marghrete. Brainstorming. The information needed to be made public, but it was too early then. All you needed to do was find a way and a perfect time. Vaccination would be a bigger problem. We had to take care that this anti-vaccine is somehow shoehorned into the official vaccination schedule. But how?

10

Karen was a very attractive black woman. She combined some of Asia, Africa and Europe. My sense of women has not betrayed me. She was the offspring of an American man with a white father and a black mother, and a Filipina. An extremely beautiful woman. But Brian's.

I rushed like a wolf to the served dinner. I didn't know what I was eating, but it was good, very good, and extremely tasty. And hunger has lowered the criteria. After dinner, Karen left us. We went to the terrace where we sat in the rocking chairs. Brian inherited a cosy house that offered comfort and homeliness. He brought a bottle of cognac with him. We lit cigars and were silent for a few moments. The host was the first to speak:

"You know, David, I've been thinking about what you told me in the afternoon. It's so crazy and life-threatening that it sent my adrenaline soaring. Not even in the craziest sci-fi scenario could I have imagined this. I knew it would happen at some point, but I didn't think it would happen in my lifetime. We have nothing else to do, we are going to war, David. Cheers."

We clinked glasses and took a sip of the excellent French cognac that Brian always had in stock. Then I said:

"Brian, I'm glad you're in this game with me, but this tragedy doesn't make me happy one bit. Do you realise that the world we knew will no longer exist. Everything has lost its meaning. What have I got to look forward to? I can only assure you that I will not surrender and that I will fall in the fight."

"Me too, my friend." We clinked glasses again. "You know, David," Brian continued. "This is our destiny, we have been called to try to save the world. The chances of success are less than one percent, but as you said, this is a war and we are on the right side."

"Which is the right side?"

"Ours, for sure. I have a plan on how we are going to tackle this crazy issue. First, we travel somewhere and from there we send out information about the nano-apocalypse, which is practically happening, to all the newsrooms of the world's major media outlets."

"I myself think it is better not to raise alarms with the masters. Let them think that they are safe for now, that the information has not escaped their bubble. Maybe it would be better to find a way to vaccinate people with our nano-cocktail."

"OK, I agree with you. Let's wait, let's prepare the ground. I suggest that we travel as soon as possible to Uganda, where my friend Monica, a doctor who worked for the World Health Organisation and now volunteers in this poor African country, is. Maybe she could help us with how to approach vaccination."

"I have to be in Whistler, Canada, on June 30th."

"Before that, we can go to Uganda. I have some money, so we can travel."

"Don't worry about money. I have enough money; the McCormacks gave it to me. From Canada, I have to go to Brazil, then to Hong Kong and finally back to Europe to visit my good friend in Copenhagen. Remember David Luiz, whom we met in Afghanistan?"

"Of course I remember him. Nice boy."

"When I was thinking about who to tell about this issue, my first thought was you, then David Luiz from Sao Paulo, Wang Shu from Hong Kong and Marghrete, a great journalist from Denmark. I would like to try to do something with you. With your ideas, with your penetrating mind and with the free spirit that adorns you, we might just find that one percent chance to make a success of the campaign."

"Excellent. I am for the cause. You can trust me too; I have at least three candidates for our group, actually four. Karen is also a journalist."

"Right, but there shouldn't be more than ten of us in a group, because then it's hard to manage and coordinate it."

"I agree. Remember Valentina, the Colombian girl I was with in Russia."

"Of course I remember her."

"Well, she is the first candidate. The next candidate is Vasili, from Petrograd, the third candidate is Yunru, from Shanghai and my Karen."

"These two women are probably your ex-lovers. Are you sure this wouldn't jeopardise our work?"

"No, not at all. On the contrary, I know all three of them very well and trust them completely. We parted amicably with Valentina and Yunru. Vasili saved my life in Russia."

"OK, if you say so. What happened in Russia?"

"Long story. Valentina and I fell into the hands of the Moscow mafia. I stupidly verbally assaulted a man in a bar, who turned out to be a high-ranking Mafia officer. I was very drunk. Against our will, three hawkers took us from the bar to an abandoned factory in the Moscow suburbs. There was a boss waiting for us, with whom we had a fight, and another man of even higher rank. The boss said I had offended him and the one with the higher rank calmly said, 'A hundred thousand dollars and we let you go or you stay here'. I sobered up immediately. Where can we get so much money? I was horrified. I will die of stupidity and take Valentina with me. When I was about to give up, I thought of Vasili, who had returned to Petrograd, and Valentina and I, after a few days' wandering around Moscow, wanted to return home. Valentina would come with me to Melbourne. I asked the kidnappers if I could call an acquaintance who could provide me with money. They allowed me to speak to him on the phone. I called Vasili and told him what had happened to us. He told us to be calm and not to challenge the kidnappers in any way and to tell them that our rescue would come the next day. It was a long night in a cold factory. We got water, nothing else. The next afternoon, Vasili showed up at the factory. The boss came to us with him and said, 'You can go, your friend saved your life'. We left the factory and sat in Vasili's old Volga. Then I asked him, 'Where did you get the money?' Vasili smiled and said that he didn't need any money and that he had used a joker he got from the mafia to get us released. When I asked him about a joker, he just smiled. Vasili was a former KGB officer, but in new Russia he was a journalist, or a man who knew everything, a Russian encyclopaedia."

"And you kept this from me."

"There was no real opportunity to tell you. Well, now I just did it."

"Let's do it."

We finished the evening with another bottle, which brought us to our knees.

11

We were planning to leave for Uganda on the 18th, and after a week in Africa we would fly to Vancouver. Two days in cold Melbourne was enough. The three of us headed west to warmer Halls Creek, where Brian had his ranch, which we could get to only by plane. Brian had an old four-seater plane parked at the airport in Halls Creek, which we flew to his ranch. We were also joined by a friend of his. I guess Brian had planned this before so that I wouldn't feel too alone in the wilderness.

If it hadn't been for the sword of Damocles overhead, those few days in Halls Creek would have been superb. Brian and I only spoke about our case once, when he told me that he had told Karen everything. She was ready to help as much as she could.

Laura and I got along great and had a lot of fun; she was a free bird who brightened up my days at the ranch. It was obvious that I brightened her days. Sex n' drugs n' Rock n' Roll.

We returned to Melbourne two days before our departure for Uganda. I liked Brian's ranch so much that I asked Brian, more as a joke, if I could live to see the end of the world there. Brian said:

"No problem dude. Here we can settle down for the autumn of life and wait for death together with our chosen ones. All we need is a cellar full of wine and other goodies in bottles."

We arrived in Entebbe in the afternoon. Monica was waiting for us at the airport. An interesting woman in her fifties, she looked younger. Not only did she share a name with Monica Bellucci, but she also looked incredibly similar to her. We sat in her Toyota and immediately drove to Masaka, south-west of Entebbe, where Monica lived and worked. Brian told her why we were visiting during the drive. At first, she thought it was all far-fetched, but then I told her the whole story again. She was stunned.

"And why did you tell me that?" she asked. I replied:

"Because we think you are one of the few people we can trust and who knows much about vaccination. As we told you, this terrible virus, these nano-monsters, can only destroy the same monsters. And these counter-robots will soon be available. We just ask you to think about it and help us as much as you can. Or you can report us to the police and get rid of us."

"Don't talk nonsense, David. I need some time to think about whether I should even get into this Eldorado with you and how I can help."

"OK," said Brian. "We'll stay here for a week, then we're off to Canada."

"Give me three days. I have a lot of work to do. I have arranged accommodation for you with friends. Pay them whatever you think it was worth. Then meet me on Tuesday evening and we'll talk. Do you agree with my proposal?"

"That is an acceptable proposal for us," I replied. Brian nodded.

The house we stayed in was Ugandan. Pure and simple. There was a fan on the ceiling of our room, making sure we didn't get too hot. Although outside temperatures were not too high either. The proximity of Lake Victoria has created perfect conditions for mosquitoes to flourish. The data on malaria in Uganda was favourable, but we still took anti-malaria pills in Melbourne. We have not been vaccinated against yellow fever. I was hoping we could get through a week without it.

We spent three days on the lake. Once we even fished with local fishermen. The Victoria lake, the water, the fish, the simple fishermen, they captivated me so much that I wanted to stay with them and fish every day. I wouldn't think about anything but fish. Beauty, peace, but inside, there was no peace for me. Brian's initial enthusiasm for the fight had also waned. We had many talks. We were looking for different ways to resist the meteor, which was hurtling towards the Earth. Again, we shared the opinion that we would give the media a try after all. But in the end, we came back to the same starting point. It was not yet time for the media. We hoped to get a fresh start with Monica.

Monica welcomed us in her house, which was even more modest than where we stayed. We sat on the veranda, which was enclosed with mosquito netting. Dinner was served by the housekeeper who was looking after Monica. Lots of vegetables, rice and meat. We drank beer. We didn't talk much during dinner. After dinner, when the housekeeper had cleared the table, Monica was the first to speak:

"Dear friends. I have made a decision. I will help you as much as I can. I do not promise that we will be successful, but if we do nothing, then we are not free-thinking people. I have thought a lot about what you told me. I have to admit, I was crushed. I can't imagine that even in the most fantastic dreams. After two days of huffing and puffing, I accepted the truth and the fact that you did not make up this story and that you did not come to Africa to tell me fairy tales and nonsense. Immediately after careful consideration, it occurred to me that Africa would be the most affected. Africans have always been at the bottom of the human scale. First a slave hunting ground for America, then slaves on their own land. When they were liberated, which never really happened, Africa became a testing ground for war games, for testing weapons, and its inhabitants became laboratory mice in the research of medicines, but also of poisons, viruses and so on. As soon as a democratic state emerges in an African country, there is a coup d'état, most often military, financed by external powers that want to continue exploiting its people and its natural wealth. They put in power cruel dictators who, with their mercenaries, are even more ruthless and cruel to their own people than white people. That is why I am convinced that Africa will not only be decimated, but perhaps completely devastated. And this has made me even more determined to do everything in my power to prevent this from happening, or to resist this terrible genocide. I hope you don't mind me taking a longer introduction and lecturing about Africa and its people."

"Not at all, Monica dear," Brian replied.

"When I first came to Africa, it felt like my long-sought home. Here I felt really safe, equal and, above all, human. It is true that there are many things in Africa that are difficult for white people to accept and understand, but they are also just people. We are barbarians too, always have been and still are. And what our masters and soul-breakers are preparing is the worst barbarism in all human history, against all human laws, against the laws of nature and against the laws of the universe. It is against the Creator, a direct attack on Him. Although I am not religious and I am not a member of any religion, I believe in equality, in goodness, in love, and I am aware that nothing can come from nothing, that every event in this world must have a cause, just as in the universe. I don't have enough time to study that now because I have a lot of work, but I know something about esoteric issues, and I know they are a vital part of human life. Maybe that's still to come.

Despite my full-time job, I will devote every spare second, every atom of myself to this holy war for people's lives. When I was thinking about how to go about defending humanity, I thought of my good friend, role model, mentor and colleague at the World Health Organisation, Dr Thomas Kendall. I've already spoken to him," I had to terminate.

"Did you mention anything to him that Brian and I told you? This could put our work and lives at risk."

"Don't be afraid. I am aware of the seriousness and the great sensitivity of this matter. I called him as a friend. We hear from each other a lot, and he calls me a lot too. I wanted to know how he was, whether he was healthy, whether he was in good shape despite his venerable years. I told him nothing about you, not even to mention anything from this criminal scenario. Mr Thomas Kendall is retired and lives alone on Vancouver Island, British Columbia, on the western part of the island in small town, Tofino, after his wife's death. Here you have his address. When you meet him, it will be enough to tell him that I am sending you to him. Then all doors will be open to you."

When Monica mentioned British Columbia, Brian and I looked at each other and smiled. That meant we were going from Whistler to Tofino.

"He will connect you to the most responsible and reliable people who are the vaccination coordinators around the world, on all continents, as well as those from the biggest countries. Through them, you will be able to distribute an anti-vaccine that will stop the killing and subjugation. Africa will be mine. The rest of the world will be on your shoulders, or in the hands of people nominated by Dr Kendall."

"Monica, we are really glad that you joined us and saved us the time and effort of trying to find a solution to introduce and distribute the anti-vaccine in the world," I said.

"Dr Kendall will have the last word. Once he confirms his consent, which I have no doubt he will, you will have a lot of travelling to do, a lot of work to do, a lot of money to spend."

"Money is not the problem," I replied.

"I would ask you, as soon as you get the vaccine, to give it to Africans first. I will immediately start action on African soil. Dr Kendall will open the channels for the vaccine to reach us."

"Hopefully soon," I said. "We'll know more as soon as we meet in Whistler. We will find a way to keep you informed about the progress of our project. We will also meet in person several times. Maybe it would not be a good idea for us to always meet here at your place. Would it be too much for you if you were to meet in, say, neighbouring countries like Kenya, Sudan, Congo or Tanzania? Not far from the border. And Brian and I will be writing articles about these countries, so we'll be coming back here."

"No, I don't see any problems. I have friends in all these countries who I know will help me with the national authorities, but also with the local authorities, so that I don't have problems crossing borders. But I'm a doctor and they are a bit less suspicious of us."

"Tomorrow, we'll bring you some money to help you get by and help us. We have plenty of money for this project. The McCormacks, the two scientists I met in Geneva, gave me enough money. We can also dedicate some money for your work here. Tell us how much you need and in a few days the money will be with you, whenever you need it."

"Thank you David, thank you Brian. There is never enough money in Africa. I would be grateful for your contribution."

"Tomorrow we will bring thirty thousand dollars in cash."

"Are you kidding me? So much money. Do you know what thirty thousand means in Africa? That is wealth. Thank you very much."

The rest of the evening we spent drinking beer and chatting. The next day, we met again at Monica's in the evening. We gave her thirty thousand dollars. Tears welled up in her eyes as she accepted them. We were also moved by her emotion.

Days to our departure to Canada we spent at the lake and on the lake. I wrote an article about Lake Victoria, about the people who lived there and for whom the lake and life in it meant their lives and their survival. Brian wrote an article about Monica's selfless medical work. By writing articles, we will not raise suspicions about the real reasons for our mass journeys. The next article will be about Whistler and its attractions.

12

We arrived in Whistler two days before the meeting with the McCormacks. In Vancouver, we rented a Ford pick-up and drove to the famous tourist and ski resorts in Western Canada. The miles were piling up. We didn't count them. We rented two rooms at the Pinnacle Hotel in the centre of Whistler. We were exploring Whistler and its surroundings and looking for topics for an article. I decided to write about tourism in Whistler, and Brian about the coexistence of bears and humans. We rented golf equipment and hit the Nicklaus North Golf Course, where we would have to meet Joseph and Kamala. The day before the planned meeting, we actually met Joseph and Kamala at a golf course where they were also playing golf. If someone had been watching and observing us, he would not have suspected that it was a chance meeting of old friends. We arranged a round of golf the next day and a late lunch at the golf course or another restaurant. Brian said:

"God is on our side."

After meeting Monica, I felt a new wind blowing through me, bringing a lot of optimism. Brian also saw the twinkle at the end of the tunnel. It was still a long way to go, and there were many obstacles ahead. Fearsome beasts have been prowling the paths of our brotherhood of nano-fighters. In the evening, we were hunters. Both were successful. We ended the day in a bar, where we bumped into two Swedish women. I woke up the next day with mixed feelings. Next to me was the blonde I shared a room with.

We arrived at the golf course half an hour before the agreed time. We didn't wait long before Joseph and Kamala arrived. We left our mobile phones at the hotel. It was a Tuesday, and according to Joseph, that was the day when there were the fewest people on the golf course. In the summer, there were a lot of Americans coming to Whistler, and people coming from other parts of the world, but that day was surprisingly quiet. Once again, God was on our side. We could talk while playing golf.

We told Joseph and Kamala what had happened before our meeting. In fact, everything important for our project had happened in the last few days. We made a breakthrough by visiting Monica in Uganda.

"What are your plans for the future?" asked Joseph.

I replied:

"First we will visit Dr Kendall on Vancouver Island, and after that meeting, we will see how it goes and then we will make a plan for the future. I originally planned to travel from Whistler to Brazil to visit a friend, then to Hong Kong and finally to Europe. We'll probably add trips to Colombia, Shanghai and Russia, where Brian's friends are. Through them, we will be able to more easily and quickly contact the people suggested by Dr Kendall, through whom we will be able to distribute vaccines with anti-robots that will prevent the hostile nanorobots from working. In Africa reception, distribution and vaccination will be organised by Ms Monica Ricchello."

"Well done, David," said Joseph, excitedly. "We have great news too. We are now well on the way to producing enough nano-robots in a few months, by early next year at the latest, that will be programmed to our commands and will effectively destroy the nano-robots that the global elite will use. We have also gained a few more trusted friends who will help us to prepare enough vaccines for the launch of the campaign in the meantime. We will continue to work to ensure that we do not run out of counter-robots. But here, again, we must be very careful. If just one link in this chain fails, we will not be able to complete this project and we will all be condemned to death."

"All of us already involved in this operation are well aware of this," said Brian. "There is no going back, and there must be no mistakes, because there can be no corrections. David has trusted me and I will justify his trust. The people I want to involve in this campaign are also trustworthy people. I put my life in their hands without any problems. We must succeed because we are on the right side."

"We may succeed in the short term, maybe even in the medium term, in slowing down this beastly depopulation and subjugation, but we cannot count on the long term. The masters will surely find a way to achieve their goals. Well, what matters now is that we work for tomorrow. What happens next week is still relatively far away."

"We're going to Dr Kendall's tomorrow." This time I spoke up. "We keep working. We want to put in place all the necessary organisation and infrastructure for an immediate action once your vaccines are available."

"Excellent," continued Joseph. Kamala was quiet all the time, but her presence, her appearance, made us calm, had a good effect on Joseph and on us. "We've sent some more money to your account. All to avoid problems on your travels and at work. Contact your bank so that you can keep track of the on-line turnover of your account. They will give you appropriate instructions on how to do this. When you're in Europe, maybe just pop into the bank in Geneva."

"Thank you Kamala, thank you Joseph. Together with our friends, we will do our best to justify your trust."

This time, Kamala spoke up:

"We knew you were the right person and we are convinced that you and your friends are the best possible choice for this job. A supernatural force has connected us to you. Through you, we are investing in humanity, in the good in this world, in the future. We have enough money."

"Thank you," I said. Brian, who felt a real, human pride in being part of this great story, also thanked them. Then Joseph spoke again:

"Kamala and I propose to meet again in four months' time, on October 26th in Tulum, on the east coast of Mexico. We have a house there and every autumn we spend some time in this beautiful place by the Caribbean Sea. Here on this slip you have the address where you can reach us. 5 pm. If you're there earlier, maybe we'll meet again by chance, like we did here in Whistler."

I took the slip of paper and put it in my pocket. We played all eighteen holes and then went into town for a late lunch. The next day, Brian and I drove out of Whistler early in the morning.

13

We drove through the picturesque Canadian countryside to Squamish, where we stopped because of Stawamus Chief. A large rock mound overlooking the city along the rugged Pacific coast was a paradise for climbers. I used to practise this sport, so I had to see this rock. I will probably never be able to afford it. In a friendly bar, we had breakfast and then explored the city, where at every turn we encountered influences and traditions of indigenous people.

"So far so good," I said to Brian.

"It looks very good. If we can reach an agreement with Dr Kendall, then we will travel around the world a bit more to set up a network through which we will distribute the vaccine."

"I'm not a pessimist, but I think everything is going too smoothly."

"Because God is on our side," said Brian, with a smile.

"Yes, but from experience in my life, there is always an obstacle somewhere, a barrier that tests my determination and my strength, whether I am ready to go all the way. Did you think that something would happen to the McCormacks or to us during the time we don't see them? What would it be then?"

"There is always a way."

"Yes, but who do we turn to if something happens to them?"

"I don't know."

"That's what I'm talking about. The matter is so devilishly dangerous and sensitive that we have no chance at all of resolving it and getting it done. We climb Stawamus Chief without ropes, without belays. One mistake, one small slip and you fall into the abyss. You shatter into nanoparticles. That started to worry me."

"We definitely need to agree with Joseph on backup options, on safeguards in case of an unforeseen situation."

"And until 26th October, pray that nothing happens to jeopardise our project."

"I'm sure everything will be fine by October 26th and we'll be soaking in the warm Caribbean Sea by then."

"I remain positive, but also cautious. We need to talk about who we can trust to take over if something happens to us. You come first, and you are with me. I also trust David Luiz, Marghrete, Wang Shu, but I don't know whether they are capable of taking this project as far as we are taking it."

"I trust Monica and Vasili. Monica will not leave Africa. Vasili is certainly a great replacement for us. Maybe we should have met him before the others."

"Right. Find out where he is and when we are done with Kendall, we'll meet him."

"Agreed."

We got in our pick-up and drove to Horseshoe Bay, where we boarded the ferry to Vancouver Island, Nanaimo. A strange premonition, an apparition, a dark cloud was always over me. I had to get rid of it because it was crippling my creativity and positivity, which we need more than anything else. I was watching the sea. The sea has always calmed me. The sea was the closest to what we imagined as eternity. The closest to space. The sea existed on Earth before we humans crawled out of it as tadpoles, and it will exist long after we crawl back into it as tadpoles. If the universe's plan is to wipe out seven billion or more people from Earth, then all our efforts are in vain. How can a group of tadpoles can defy the universe? How can we stop the flow of an inevitable fate that is stronger than all the tadpoles on Earth put together? How can we resist the force that created us, together with the known and unknown universe? Yin and yang, light and darkness, the dualism that rules the universe. Without one, there is no other. The planet has come to a time when it is on the dark side of the moon, in the shadow of the black substance that has spilled between us and our life-giving star, the source of life. But if we are part of the universe, then surely our role in this world is not just to play an extra, to eat, reproduce and sleep. We possess the mind, which is surely our strongest attribute. We do not defy nature, the universe, with it, but with its help organise our lives so that we can survive as easily as possible on this dusty particle of the universe. The self-proclaimed masters of the planet are defying the universe and it is our sacred duty to resist this, to resist the darkness that has begun to devour us.

This was the conclusion I came to as I leaned on the railing of the deck of a large ferry, staring out to sea. We landed in Nanaimo, got in the car and drove to Tofino, which was on the other side of the big island. We arrived there in the late afternoon. We found spare rooms in a small hotel near where Dr Kendall lived. We planned to visit him the following morning. We enjoyed a tour of Tofino and dinner at sunset on the terrace of an interesting restaurant by the ocean. During dinner, I was watching an interesting elderly gentleman, gazing fixedly into the distance towards Japan with a glass of white wine. Something about him attracted me. He was certainly an interesting man.

The next day, at 10 am, we rang the door of a small house by the sea. We were answered by the same grey-haired gentleman in a big white T-shirt and denim shorts that we met in the restaurant the night before.

"Dr Kendall?" I asked.

"Yes, and you are?"

"David Mlinar and Brian Koukuris. Your friend Monica Ricchello referred us to you."

"Monica," exclaimed Dr Kendall, excitedly. "Please come in."

Through a small entrance hall and a large, bright lounge, we were ushered towards a glass door leading to a spacious terrace near the sea. After serving us the tea, he had been drinking on the terrace before we arrived, he sat down next to us and we started discussion. We asked him to get rid of the phones. Dr Kendall sympathetically put the phone off and took it to the house. When he came back, he asked:

"Tell me how dear Monica is, have you seen her recently?" Brian replied:

"We were with her in Uganda ten days ago."

"Wonderful. How is my dear friend?"

"Good. She is committed to her work. She lives for the people she can help."

Brian then told his story of how he and Monica met and became friends. Then it was my turn. He introduced me.

"Excellent," said Dr Kendall. "Monica must have told you our story."

"Yes." This time I spoke up.

"I suppose you must have something important to tell me if you've flown to me from Africa?"

"Yes," I continued. "We have come to you with a great request, Dr Kendall."

I told him the whole story of the nano-robots, without names, but with all the important events that followed from the moment I fell into it. Dr Kendall listened with interest, his gaze now and then fixed on the sea. When I finished, he said:

"I was afraid of that. Sooner or later, someone would have thought of trying something like that. You say that there is hope for humanity and that I can be part of that hope. It is certainly a difficult task, extremely difficult. But it is possible. I need a few days to check my options. And as I see it, the only possible communication is a direct meeting. This complicates matters, but I fully understand that we need to ensure maximum safety. So I will ask you to stay in Tofino for a few more days."

"We don't see any problems," said Brian. "There are certainly many things we can do here."

"Certainly, dear guests. Where are you staying? Nearby? You could be with me too."

"No, we don't want to disturb your rhythm of life," I said.

"As you wish. It wouldn't bother me. Maybe I would have disturbed you. I invite you to go fishing on Monday. I have a small boat and the three of us can go out on the open sea. There, at sea, we will have a smooth discussion about how we proceed further. By then, I will certainly have a plan on how we will tackle this project."

"We'd be happy to join you," I replied.

"Agreed. At 6 am, my place. The weather will be wonderful."

We sat and talked for a while. He apologised for not being able to invite us to lunch because he had already arranged to have lunch with his friends.

The days in Tofino were wonderful. We could relieve the pressure that was pressing us to the ground with days like this. We rented a canoe and paddled around paradise on earth. We enjoyed it. The day before fishing with Dr Kendall, we went to sea with two American women. We needed that for our well-being too. On Monday, we were at Dr Kendall's at 6 am sharp. We drove with his car to a small harbour, where we boarded the boat. After almost two hours of sailing, we anchored off the coast on the south side of Vargas Island, near Moser Point. The coast was uninhabited. We settled into the armchairs on the stern and threw our baits into the sea. Each with his fishing rod in hand, we started the conversation.

"This is a great salmon fishery. I hope Neptune will be kind to us and provide us with a good dinner."

We just smiled and let Dr Kendall talk.

"I have taken the time I have here to look into the possibilities of a solution to this problem. I'm sorry to tell you right from the start that you will have to travel a lot."

"We are ready because we know there is no other option," I said.

"I will give you a list of people to visit this evening. These are all reliable people who can take care of the distribution of vaccines in different parts of the world. In Africa, Monica will take care of that, and that is where I see the least problems with vaccinating people. In Africa, our vaccine can be mixed in with other vaccines used to vaccinate the population against yellow fever, cholera, tetanus and many other diseases that are fought on this poor continent. The same would be elsewhere in less developed parts of the world. Whereas in the developed world, this is more problematic. We will have to wait for the mass vaccination of the population against the virus sown by the masters of the world, as you call them. The delivery of vaccines to individual centres could also be a problem. But you will deal with these people, whom I will recommend to you. And I will be at your disposal if there would be a problem anywhere. If necessary, I can also travel to where you need me. Maybe you know when the first vaccine is expected?"

"We will find out at the end of October when we meet the gentleman who will provide us with the vaccine. Probably not until early next year," I replied.

"Then we have plenty of time. To avoid meeting too often and, as a result, being at greater risk of being traced, I recommend that you speak to these people after your meeting with the gentleman, when you know when the vaccine will be available. In the meantime, I will take another look at everything and prepare what I can without jeopardising the project. What do you say to that?"

Brian replied, "We agree. We definitely agree."

"Then you don't need this list. Visit me after your meeting in October. I look forward to your visit and we can finalise our strategy for the future. I can also fly to wherever you want me to go. I admit I enjoy it here, but every now and then I have a desire to travel."

I hesitated for a few moments whether to tell him about Tulum or not. Of course we told him, because we were a team.

"We will be in Tulum, Yucatan, Mexico, for a few days from October 26th. If it's not too difficult for you, we can meet there," I said.

"Great, we'll meet there."

"Right. We will stay here for at least a few more days to make a plan for the future and to suggest when and where we could meet there."

"You can come to me any time. In two days, we can go to the sea again. I know where the orcas are gathering, if you're interested."

We were given a topic for a report from Tofino. The float on the line of Brian's rod sank into the water. He pulled a hefty salmon on board. Dinner was taken care of. At three o'clock, we weighed anchor and sailed back. We wanted to go to our hotel to freshen up before dinner, but Dr Kendall offered to do it at his place. He grilled a delicious salmon on the terrace and served it with interesting plants from the sea. We also drank a delicious Canadian white wine, a superb Pinot Blanc, produced on the mainland not far from Vancouver.

We stayed in Tofino for a few more days. We agreed that there was no need to involve the rest of our friends in the project, because we would be able to contact and work directly with the people Dr Kendall would propose without intermediaries. The fewer people involved in the case, the greater the level of security. We decided to include only the versatile Vasili in the project, who could be of great help to us. We would give him everything he needs to replace us if anything unforeseen happens to us. Brian contacted Vasili. He was on the Adriatic. He said we could visit him in Dalmatia, or he could come wherever we wanted. We decided to travel from Tofino to my home in Slovenia. I suggested to Brian to invite Karen, I'd invite Beti, and we could all go to Dalmatia together and take a long break. Brian agreed. We had an interesting autumn waiting for us and all seasons ahead, so we decided to go to sea for a while. Then Karen and Brian would return to Australia before travelling to Mexico. Dr Kendall made for a wonderful day at sea. For the first time in my life, I saw orcas in the wild. The rugged coastline of the surrounding uninhabited islands and islets beckoned the orcas and us who wanted to meet them. In one of the picturesque little bays, we found a great shelter where we had lunch from the sea.

"Dear friends, since we first met, my day begins and ends with what you have told me. I think a lot about the different scenarios that could happen. There are many opportunities for success, just as there are opportunities for the opposite. I decided to be even more active than I had originally planned. I will help you wherever you need me. It is a great challenge for me, and a great satisfaction that even now, as a pensioner, I can contribute my share to the well-being of humanity. If you need me, I can join you to discuss and organise individual vaccine distribution campaigns, once we know when to expect the first shipments. The whole of the Americas, both North and South, including all the Pacific you can leave to me. On other continents, you will be able to work with people I consider one hundred percent reliable. What is your opinion?"

I replied:

"A welcome offer from you, Dr Kendall. With your help, we will definitely be faster and more efficient, giving us an even better chance of ultimate success. From Mr and Mrs McCormack" This was the first time I had mentioned their names, because I had decided that it was right that Dr Kendall knew who was behind it at all. "I have received a substantial sum of money that can fund all the necessary actions to carry out our project. In short, financial support is available."

"I don't need money. My late wife and I saved enough for our old age. We didn't have any children, so money is not a problem. Instead, give this money to Monica, who desperately needs it. I hope you gentlemen agree with me?"

"Monica will be delighted with your generous gift," replied Brian.

"I will arrive in Tulum on 25th October. I managed to book the Maria Del Mar hotel by the sea, near Tulum, online. You can reach me there or leave a message."

"Maria Del Mar. Did you remember the name of the hotel, Brian?" I asked him. "Written in the brain. Maria Del Mar."

"I've already bought my plane ticket," continued Dr Kendall. "If I don't manage to be there, I'll probably get sick or join my wife. I have also taken care of such cases. I will leave a list of people who will help us with my friend in Seattle. I will give you her address when we get home. I always think in two tracks. Nothing can stop us. I also took care of the third rail. The list will also be with Monica, and I will send it to her together with a shipment of medicines that we are preparing for her together with our former colleagues at the World Health Organization. Before that, I will have general discussions with my friends who will be on the list, without any mention of anything that might disclose us."

This meticulous organisation of Dr Kendall amazed me and made me wonder whether we would all survive until the Tulum meeting. We will make sure that Vasili is included in this odyssey. The McCormacks will also have to find a way to keep the project going no matter what happens to them.

We returned to the port before dark. We ended the evening in the restaurant where we met for the first time. I told Dr Kendall that we saw him there the first evening we arrived in Tofino.

"An invisible force watches over us because we are fighting for the right thing." Dr Kendall smiled. After dinner, we went to his house where he gave us a few bottles of Pinot Blanc and the address of a friend of his in Seattle. We said goodbye until we met each other again in Tulum.

14

We flew from Vancouver to Frankfurt, where we planned to stay for three days. In Wiesbaden, we visited our mutual friend Heinz, a journalist who was an expert on big corporate affairs. We wanted to give him a bit of a shake-up regarding nanotechnology and the multinationals behind it. He has certainly come across this issue and probably has information that would be useful to us. He welcomed us at his home.

"Hey, where are you two from?" Brian replied:

"We're from Western Canada, where we did some reporting together. And you? Still spying on big companies?"

"I don't spy," Heinz cut in loudly. "I look under their fingers, as far as they allow me."

"You've been doing a lot with Siemens lately?" I joined the conversation.

"Siemens and Bayer have occupied me for more than two years. Something is happening, but I can't fully decipher the signals coming from there."

"What signals?" Brian wondered.

"I don't know what that means exactly, but there has been a lot of cooperation between them recently. A tech and a pharma giant are up to something. I have a theory, but what is really going on, I don't have a real answer to that yet."

It was clear to Brian and me what these two mega companies were doing. Nanotechnology and pharmaceuticals are teaming up to carry out a conspiracy whose goals were entrusted to me by the McCormacks which had completely changed my life and Brian's too.

"Tell me more about it," I said to Heinz.

"As a journalist, I attended an international conference of big technology companies in Tokyo, where they were discussing how to work together and how to divide the world. At the same time, a meeting of the world's leading pharmacists was held in Kobe. I have seen very lively communication between

Kobe and Tokyo. It was not only Bayer and Siemens that met, but representatives of other technology and pharmaceutical companies also met frequently. But at the time I did not attribute this of any particular importance. I thought they were just meeting as a courtesy and protocol, because they were all in Japan at the same time. But when I returned home and continued to spy on Siemens, I soon realized the continuation of intensive communication between Siemens and Bayer. What's more, Siemens teams of experts have gone to Bayer and vice versa. Then, in Strasbourg, I met an old friend and colleague, Friderick from Le Monde, who told me an interesting theory about the collaboration between pharma and high-tech."

"Tell us." We wanted to know.

"Long story, I'll invite you to the pub for dinner and tell you all about it."

Despite our tiredness, we accepted his invitation because we were very interested in what he had to say. We went to a nearby pub, where they had excellent beer of their own, tapped from wooden barrels. The pub was very old and looked rather shabby and neglected, but the beer and the great food made it look like a noble restaurant. After a great dinner, accompanied by mugs of clear beer, Heinz picked up where he left off, in Strasbourg.

"Frederick and I spent a few hours thinking about what this collaboration between technologists and pharmacists means. He told me an interesting story about a microscopic technology called nanotechnology. In Russia, it is believed that as early as the end of the last millennium, microscopically tiny devices have been injected into the human body. These devices are supposed to circulate around the body and repair any defects they find in it. So instead of surgeries being performed by surgeons, these devices would perform these operations at a microscopic level. Science fiction. He claimed to have heard about it in the year two thousand, when was in Cyprus, where he met a Russian general, a former KGB officer. He told him in confidence that he had witnessed experiments carried out by Russian scientists, paving the way for the future of medicine. Frederick devoted himself to further research in nanotechnology. Since then, science is said to have made huge strides in this field. In fact, nanotechnology is already present in everyday life. The last time I went to a car wash, it worked on the principle of nanoparticles, which cleaned my car. Friderick has given me a lot of information and told me about the nano world, but after meeting him, I put that nano shit on the back burner. But I soon came back to this theory because it made the most sense when I saw the integration of pharmacy and high technology. Then I also delve deeper into this sphere. Whether this is really about the use of nanotechnology in pharmaceuticals, I do not have a reliable answer. I could write articles on this, but I have nothing to go on except speculation, which has arisen since the intense communication between Bayer and Siemens began. I wanted to get information from Siemens management and also from Bayer, but they both politely refused. Is it nano-cooperation between them or something else, I have no answer. All I know is that something is happening."

"Interesting," Brian spoke up. "Have you learned anything else about this technology?"

"No, just speculation. Maybe even NATO has a hand in this, like the military in Russia. If the military is involved, then this technology will be used to destroy and kill rather than to heal. Have you heard anything about nanotechnology?"

I replied. I didn't want to expose myself too much, so I was more diplomatic. Heinz was an OK boy, but Brian and I didn't know him well enough to trust him with our mission.

"I know very little about it. I have heard that nanotechnology exists, but what exactly that means, I have no idea. There will probably be more on this in the future. Have you heard anything more, Brian?"

"No, I have no idea. Just like you, I've heard and nothing else."

"Well, boys, there's a lot more to write about. I am convinced that this is the technology of the future. Like all great inventions up to now, they are first tested by the army in war, and here, imagination knows no bounds. Nano-soldiers can kill many more people than all conventional weapons combined, and compared to nuclear weapons; an attacker is not at risk. We are all at risk if an atomic bomb explodes, but a nano-army can only precisely destroy specific targets. Can you imagine dropping these little devices into drinking water to hit specific targets? For example, on anyone who might be diabetic, or hypertensive? They find a weak point in each of us that they can attack. They can attack your brain, digestive organs, sexual organs, nervous system. Whatever pops into their head?

I know it sounds like science fiction, but with these madmen running the world, anything is possible. In Venezuela, Chavez was reportedly given cancer by the CIA, which caused his death. In a sense, they have released nanoparticles into his body, which killed him."

Our friend told us a lot. This was a reminder to us that there is a lot of information about nanotechnology circulating in the world and that there are a lot of people interested in it. This is why the main players are and will continue to be even more cautious and will monitor everyone and anyone who will be involved. Maybe Heinz is already being followed and is already on the list of the various intelligence services responsible for law and order. We hoped we hadn't made a mistake by visiting him. That's why I said:

"I'm not interested in this nano-shit. I have so many other things on my to-do list."

"I'm not interested in that at the moment either," Brian continued. "Although it sounds very tempting, I have a lot of other work to do. Go ahead, Heinz. There will certainly be a lot of talk about it in the future, and as a result, a large crowd of curious journalists and other researchers will take up this phenomenal discovery."

After a few mugs, we went back to Heinz. At first, we were going to spend the night in his big house, but after an evening in the pub, we decided it was wiser to go to a hotel than to stay with him. His departure to Hamburg in the morning was also in our favour. We found a hotel and decided to fly to Ljubljana the next day if possible, as we had originally planned a three-day stopover in Germany. The next morning, we managed to get free seats on a flight to Ljubljana.

15

My mother was delighted to see us. She was even happier for Brian than for me, whom she really loved. Before Karen came to Slovenia, I let them drink wine and talk. I met with Beti the very next day. Something pinched and stung in my stomach, I had to see her. This time I found it extremely beautiful and attractive. Have I fallen in love with her, I wondered. Does it mean to me more than I allow myself to admit. I really longed for her. She has been in my thoughts many times, even when I was travelling. Sometimes I wondered what she was doing at that moment when I thought of her. Has she found a partner? Does she sleep with many men? All too often, such thoughts have crossed my mind. But who am I to worry about what happens to her? She often showed her affection for me in the most direct way, but all I saw were her big breasts and her nice ass. She was my sex buddy when I was at home. Just sex, nothing else. But she was all about me, hoping that maybe one day I would love her. And that day has clearly arrived. This time I wanted her hug, her kiss, more than her body. Why would I lie to myself? Maybe it's time to settle down and get on with it. But the future that lay ahead did not give me hope that we could live together. But my future is the same as hers. We can have it together, or neither of us will have it at all. What will happen if I die, if I am killed? I had a rational answer for that at the time too. Death is always with us. Once you accept that, its presence in your daily life doesn't bother you. If I am endangering her life because of what I am doing, because I want to be with her now, then I must not attract her to me. But what is left? If they expose me, they will expose everyone. The rebellion will be stopped and crushed. Not because of me, but because the masters of the world will be even more careful to get rid of anyone who has been involved in the nano-conspiracy. And then what will happen to Beti? She will be murdered or turned into a robot, a slave. If she wants to be with me, then I want to be with her. We will live together and we will die together, if that is what she wants. I decided to confess to her.

She sat motionless next to me and listened to me. I told her everything; I didn't hold anything back. When I finished, she was silent for a few moments, then she hugged me and said, with tears in her eyes:

"I knew it would happen, that one day I would be yours and you would be mine. That's why I insisted. You have been my love since the first day I met you."

I remained silent, tears creeping down my cheeks. I hugged her tighter and pulled her to me. I said the words I thought I would never say:

"I love you, Beti."

"I love you, David."

Then we squeezed our bodies together for a few minutes. I felt her warmth, her slight trembling at the happiness that had befallen her. I could feel her heart beating, which had long been there for me. Incredible happiness filled me. I felt like I was in heaven. If that's the way it is in heaven, then that's where I wanted to go. With her.

Then came the second part of our meeting. Questions, questions, questions. I answered them calmly and clearly.

"What are the chances of succeeding in what you are doing?"

"There are chances, but whether the chances of success are more than fifty percent, I don't know. I am sure it is at least fifty percent. There are still a lot of things to do, but so far everything is going better than expected."

"What will happen to you if you are found out?"

I didn't want to lie to her:

"Then my life will be worth nothing. They will get rid of me. They will probably get rid of everyone I have been in contact with in the last year. I'm sorry I got you involved."

"But I am happy. Even if I don't fully understand everything, I'm glad to be with you."

We hugged again. Then the question again: "When are you leaving again?"

"Soon. When Brian's friend Karen comes, we all go to the Adriatic together." She lowered her eyes and remained silent.

"Are you going with me?" I asked her. She nodded and burst into tears.

"I'll go if you take me with you. I'm going to the end of the world with you."

A few days later, Karen flew to Brnik. All three of us met her at the airport. Before we left for the summer in Dalmatia, we enjoyed a wander around Slovenia's hills, lakes, forests, towns, villages and famous wine cellars. Karen was enthusiastic about Slovenia; Brian had visited her before. Beti fit in perfectly. She was completely different from the Beti I knew. She used to be quiet and melancholic, but now she was lively, talkative, and fun; a completely different woman, for my sake; so I promised myself to try to be better, for her sake.

We have pushed nano-conspiracy into the subconscious. We didn't even talk about it. It emerged now and then, but only for a while. I wanted to enjoy life now, at this moment. What the future would bring, I left to its choice and did not want to burden my head with it. Beti flourished, Brian and Karen were enjoying themselves. Those were unforgettable days. We had fun in a mountain hut on Kriška Gora, supervised drinking in a wine cellar in Marezige near Koper, meeting bears in Kočevski Rog, swimming in the cold Soča, jumping in a twin from an aeroplane, pottering around Ljubljana. We were fooling around and having fun like it was the last time. My mother and her friend joined us on our wine venture. After ten days, our rejoicing was interrupted by a call from Vasili. He asked when we were coming, because it was going to be a fortnight, he had to return to Moscow. We decided to leave the next day for Split.

16

Dalmatia with Beti, probably the best time of my life. From the moment we got in the car until we got out of the car and drove back home, it was unforgettable, romantic and cinematic. I fell in love. For the first time in my life, I was in love. I fell in love with a woman who had waited all my adult life to soften me up and finally see her. Suddenly I was as soft as a goose down pillow. It made me forget the nightmare I had been living with for the last months. I don't know where Cupid came from, who shot an arrow at me that shook every cell in me and took over all my thoughts. My old friend, Beti, had become my love. Is this enlightenment before the end, I wondered.

I left the helm to Brian, with Karen sitting next to him. Beti and I sat at the back, holding hands. She shone. She got what she was waiting for. What have I been waiting for all these years? Beti? A question that had no easy answer. I was enjoying life, or at least I thought I was enjoying a life that should have had no room for Beti. Women came and went. Did I really enjoy it, or was it just a pleasure for my needs, which had evaporated by the next evening? But she was waiting for me. I have to be honest with myself, I have to admit, I thought about her all the time. But I was dissolving the thought of Beti in other women. I had to hunt and collect trophies. How masculine. Is it? Was I afraid of a relationship? I was afraid of a human being who gave me so much and I only took. The few days a year when I was at home, I was with her. That's when I took what she kept for me.

We decided to drive slowly, along the old Adriatic Highway, the Balkan Route 66. We made our first stop in Opatija, where we had our first swim. We enjoyed being adolescents going to sea alone for the first time. It was all spontaneous, without plans, without long-winded agreements. Swim, swim. Eat, eat. To love, to love. Drink, drink. Have fun, have fun. Sleep, sleep. Opatija was very nice and completely different, more colourful, livelier than all the previous

Opatijas I have been to. The sea was bluer and the fish tasted more delicious than usual. We stayed there that day.

The next day we decided to board a ferry in Rijeka and take the sea road to Split. It was a long voyage, but it went by in a flash. We rented a sailboat in Split. Brian was a good skipper. Early in the morning, we sailed to Lastovo, where Vasili was waiting for us. We arrived to the island Hvar, where we stopped again and indulged ourselves in the sea, wine and sex. Before evening the next day, we landed in Skrivena Luka on the island Lastovo. Vasili was there with his boat and his companion Irina. We got fairly drunk on it.

Then we sailed together for three days on his much bigger boat, entrusted to him by a wealthy friend. In the evening of the first day, the women went ashore and we stayed on the boat at the berth in Sobra on the island Mljet.

"I see you're enjoying yourself, Vasili?" started Brian.

"You only live once. I don't know what tomorrow holds, so I have to enjoy today. As I see, you are not suffering either." Vasili laughed.

"No," Brian replied. "As you say, we don't know what tomorrow holds. That's why David and I came to you."

We told him everything, from start to finish. We needed someone we could trust and who could replace us if necessary. The project has not to stop, no matter what happened. We were always walking on the edge of a precipice, but we had to go forward. Vasili understood everything we told him and was willing to help us.

"Of course, I want to be there. In fact, I consider it an honour and a privilege that you chose me. Is there any indication of when the big bang, the viral contamination of the planet, might be about to happen?"

I replied:

"Unfortunately, we don't know, but with practically everything in place for a final solution, we can expect it to happen very soon, perhaps as early as next year."

"If you need help delivering and distributing your vaccine in Russia and in other countries of the former Soviet Union, you can absolutely count on me."

"Of course, we're counting on you," said Brian.

"You know, Brian, that all doors are open to me," he said, smiling mischievously. Brian smiled too, but more sourly.

"You can also count on me in the preparations for the campaign. If you think it's worthwhile, I can join you in Mexico."

"Yes, if you have the chance, we'd love you to join us. We will introduce you to Joseph and Kamala, and to Dr Kendall as our deputy. If something unforeseen happens to us, you can jump in and replace us, without the need for prior typing and checking. Especially for Joseph and Kamala, this is important," I replied. "How are you with money?"

"Don't worry. This is not a problem. I would like to know whether you have made sure that any link in the chain can be replaced if problems emerged."

"Unfortunately, this is a matter that we will have to resolve with Kamala and Joseph in Tulum. While Dr Kendall has made sure that we can carry on without him. In case something happens to him, of course," I said.

"This house that you are building, and that we will build together from now on, is so fragile that it can be blown away by a little stronger breeze. Intelligence services around the world are certainly keeping a very close watch on this matter. I'm sure they follow all the people who have been involved in this project in any way. We have to be very careful when we meet the McCormacks in Mexico. Every step is controlled. The global elite will not allow anything to jeopardise their operation. Nothing is safe enough. Even when you think you're perfectly safe, you have to be careful and keep checking all aspects of safety."

"We are well aware of that," said Brian. "As a former KGB officer, you will be a great help to us to make our security even better."

"Of course, boys. The first step towards greater security and continuity of operations is to never travel together. You two also have to travel separately. Of course, you can get together and have a holiday together, like now. But even on holiday, you need to keep one eye on what's going on around you and one ear always on the frequency that catches unusual and unexpected noises and voices. Unfortunately, we will never have peace again. Even if we succeed with the vaccination campaign, it will only postpone the implementation of their project. When they sense that something is not going as planned, they will unleash their dogs to search and sniff every corner of the world."

"Do you think our efforts to vaccinate people with our vaccine are futile and completely fruitless?" I asked.

"No, I don't think so. If I had thought so, I would have said *hasta la vista muchachos* and kept on drinking wine. I want to say that we will have to be very innovative, always one step ahead, very patient and very careful. They may think there is something wrong with their nano-robots and look for possible faults. When they discover that it was a diversion, they will decide on a new strategy, a new weapon. I hope that by then a lot of time will have passed and that divine providence will warn us in time of a new danger," said Vasili, looking up at the night sky and crossing himself three times.

"I have also been thinking about what is the point of resistance when you know that the chance of success is less than one percent. But I don't want to die without a fight," I said.

"We won't give up, won't we Brian? Let's raise our glasses and toast. We drink this glass to confirm our intention to persevere in this war to the end. To final victory or to a heroic death on the battlefield," said Vasili in a tone that was a mix of sarcasm, determination, autosuggestion and drunkenness.

We needed encouragement and all that goes with it. Without determination and persistent care for its well-being, without the daily sarcastic spots, the moral would have had to fall. We were saving the world. There was no way back.

I didn't sleep well that night. We drank a fair bit of alcohol and it spoiled my sleep. By the time the girls came back, we were snoring in our own corners, and then I more or less was awake all night.

We sailed together for two more days and enjoyed the warm Mediterranean sun and cool off in the Adriatic Sea. Beti and I were one. I wasn't thinking about the future, I wasn't thinking about the nano-apocalypse that was out there somewhere. Nevertheless, its presence kept reverberating in my subconscious and it was unfathomable and unimaginable that something so beautiful, so unique, this nirvana I was experiencing at that time, could be forever interrupted by a catastrophe of unimaginable proportions, triggered not by the universe but by a group of self-proclaimed gods on Earth.

We said goodbye to Vasili and Irina. For three more weeks, the four of us lived a fairy tale, sailing from island to island, from bay to bay, from port to port. We stopped for a few days in Dubrovnik. Karen and Brian were delighted, as was Beti, who was there for the first time. Not once had there been a disagreement, a misunderstanding or anything that had disturbed the atmosphere and harmony between us. I could even say that we spoke to each other telepathically. Each of us had always known what others wanted and expected. They left the route to me, who knew the Adriatic best, while Brian handled the navigation professionally. We also had good weather. No one got seasick.

When we returned home, the weather had already started to change. The cold autumn was knocking on the door. After a few days, Brian and Karen travelled home to Australia. We agreed to come to Tulum together in October. I would go there with Beti. I decided that I would never go anywhere without her again. I felt I was a better person in every way with her. I needed a partner and a peaceful refuge, which I got with her.

17

The days until our departure for Mexico passed quickly. We were always together, with Beti. She no longer worked in the family business, but lived with my mother and me. My mother also enjoyed this new chapter in my life. We didn't talk about the future, but she definitely thought I would finally settle down and live a normal life. Although I am sure that for her, normal did not mean the kind of life which most couples live in the world. For her, it was more normal that I wouldn't travel as much as I used to and that we would be together more often, as mother and son. The autumn of life was knocking at her door and she had no one else but me.

I would not have mentioned this period before our departure to Tulum in my writing if something very unusual had not happened to me, something that frightened, shocked and marked me.

Late in the evening, Beti and I drove back from a day trip in Prekmurje. Just a few hundred metres from my house in Trstenik, near Kranj, on a road between fields and meadows, I noticed a dark shadow by the side of the road. Even now, as I write this, the hairs on my body stand on end when I remember that evening. I immediately got an uncomfortable feeling, a cold sweat washed over me, as if someone had poured a bucket of cold water over me. Beti slept next to me, I was alone. Just before I passed the shadow, it turned to me. I saw a dead-white face, black eye sockets with no eyes, a mouth with no lips; only a thin line gave a clue where it would be. An unknown force turned the steering wheel and drove over the shadow, which disappeared in a split second. I pulled off the road and into a meadow. I fainted for a moment. When I came to, Beti was writhing and moaning next to me. As the car bounced across the lawn, she hit her head on the door glass, half asleep. I helped her out of the car. She asked me:

"What happened?"

"I don't know, maybe I fell asleep for a moment." I didn't want to tell her about the apparition that got me off the road. Thank God we didn't suffer any other injuries apart from the bump on her head. We got back in the car and drove home.

That night, I was awake. I thought about what had happened, what I had seen, what it was on the side of the road that had caused me to fly off it. I wasn't drunk, I wasn't asleep, and I wasn't drugged. Hallucination? Subconscious pressures of events in my mind? I was composed. What did I see? I drove over the apparition, but nothing was felt. Am I crazy? Am I mad? I wondered what was happening to me. I couldn't come up with a rational explanation, I couldn't find an answer to the question whether I really saw something or it was just an illusion. My mind rejected any supernatural phenomenon. Something was there by the roadside. But what? If Beti hadn't been asleep, maybe she would have seen that awful apparition. Or maybe it was just a film in my head, which, after Geneva, found itself in the grip of irrational events. Human nature is mysterious, but even more mysterious is the force that created us and the universe, and we have no way of knowing what it is. I fell asleep in the morning.

I haven't said anything to anyone, not even my mother, with whom I can talk about anything. I came across an interesting book that I downloaded from the web on my Kindle, Terrorism and Illuminati in English. I read it in one piece, at night, because, despite some historical shortcomings, it attracted me to such an extent that I did not give up reading until the end of the book. The history of the Lords of the World was described in the book. There have been several theories as to where they came from, for which I would have thought, until yesterday, that these were just children's fairy tales. But it doesn't even matter whether they are fallen angels who have come to Earth from another world, or merely highly intelligent beings who have come from another planet and subjugated earthlings. It all started in Babylon. It was the centre of the world. It was there that the newcomers established their rule on Earth. It is unknown where the Sumerians, who mixed with the Semites, came from and who are thought to have brought civilization to the area. They had their own script, a language that has no common root with any language of the time. A people that was different from the Acadians and Amorites, who also lived there. There are many Sumerian cuneiform records describing the events of the time, but they are hidden from the public eye. They are said to be gods who rode in flying steel chariots, lording it over the people, and so on, to this day. It's just that we don't see them today, or they are no different from us. The Bible also says that the sons of God went to the daughters of men, took them as wives, and they bore them children. The greatest enemy of the masters, however, was religion. People were not allowed to think about goodness and love, about the immense universe of which we are a part. They had to live in fear to be ruled. Wherever people have established their authority, the masters gradually took it over. As well as religion. According to the author of this book, the Israelites lost their faith in exile in Babylon in the sixth and fifth centuries before Jesus. From then on, religion became an end in itself, working not for the good of the people but to control them. It had further alienated the people from free thought and expression. Jesus is said to have come two thousand years ago to correct the deviation. The Christian religion was born and destroyed three hundred years later when the Roman Emperor, Constantine, declared it the state religion. It was also then that the Lords finally took over Christianity, which, although it could not be broken, seven hundred years later, it was split in half between the eastern and the western part, and five hundred years later, the western part of Christianity was also divided. Rome is said to have been ruled by the subjects of the lords until today. The Islamic religion was divided and destroyed immediately after the death of Muhammad, who also came to earth to bring people back to the right path. The lords then ruled the known world in Europe and the Middle East. They made sure that their blood flowed in the rulers. Their guards are supposed to be Jews who were subjugated by the Sumerians in Babylon and mixed with them. They have been chosen as God's people. The final subjugation of the Jews came when the Israelites were exiled in Babylon in the sixth century before Jesus.

Since then, they have been the first and the chosen. Ashkenazi Jews lead the way in this. Towards the end of the Middle Ages and the beginning of the modern era, however, the rulers spread their influence across continents. First, the Americas were enslaved. China and Japan were a hard nut to crack. They subjugated India and the East Indies, and through them, put pressure on China. They were helped by Christian missionaries who spread the Christian faith by the sword and the Bible. They wanted the gold that the Chinese had got from centuries of the Silk Road. In the meantime, they had invaded Australia. The Chinese were enslaved by opium sold for gold, or sold cheap products made in India. But China was big. That is why, in the nineteenth century, they focused on Japan and completely subjugated it in just a few years, from 1862 to 1867. They have turned a feudal society into an industrial country. The film, The Last Samurai, is a correct depiction of the events of that time. They have made Japan a bridgehead for an attack on China. The Second World War was supposed to be a game played by the masters, just like the First, to increase their influence. The Japanese plundered China during World War II. They were rewarded for their work and did not have to pay war reparations to the occupied countries. The gold stolen by the Japanese from the Chinese and other East Asian nations was mostly confiscated by the Americans after the war. During the war in Singapore, the Japanese melted gold into gold bars and then hid it in underground warehouses in the Philippines. The warehouses were built by prisoners of war who, when their work was finished, were imprisoned alive underground with their guards together and the entrance was filled with explosives. Apparently, not all of Japan's gold deposits have been discovered to this day, so it is possible to see many elderly Japanese people roaming the Philippine soil with metal detectors. But they had not yet brought China to its knees after the Second World War. That is why the Communist revolution happened to them. The gold the Chinese had left was taken by the US Federal Reserve, which, in reality, was a private bank. Fearing the Communists, the wealthy Chinese gave their gold to the Americans, who issued bonds for it, but refused to recognise it fifty years later. This was still the case until today. And here I was reminded of Brian and his words about the late Polish President, Kaczynski. Finally, mighty China had also fallen under the rule of the world's masters, where they ruled through their communist proxies, and in the so-called democracies through democrats elected by the people in free elections. Russia was subjugated by the October Revolution. Stalin may have interrupted their plans, but since the revolution, Russia had been more or less under the protectorate of the masters. Something similar was happening with Putin, but insiders said it was just a game. The French Revolution was also only about seizing power, because they failed to rule through their blood-appointees here and there, just as in Tsarist Russia. The global elite today should completely dominate the world. If Venezuela happens to them, then they immediately ostracise it. Wars, revolutions, coups, terrorism, all their work to sow fear and plunder what wealth is left in some respective countries. Their goal was one country with one government, one religion and a select few slaves. Five hundred million. Freemasons, various clubs, associations, alliances, including the United Nations, the European Union, the NATO pact, trade agreements and so on, all of this is purely and simply for control and enslavement. The Warsaw Pact had a common root with the NATO Pact and with recent terrorism. The intelligence services of the world worked for them, the national armies under the Covenants worked for them, the governments of the countries worked for them. The disobedient were punished, like Iran, Iraq, Syria, Libya, Venezuela, and North Korea.

When I read this book, it was clear to me that we were living in the last period of the world revolution, when the masters would completely enslave the Earth and carry out a cosmic genocide. That's why they used nanotechnology. They have plundered the Earth, they have enslaved nations, religion, science, and they had absolutely all the levers for total world domination. The end of the world. According to Malachi's prophecy, Francis would be the last Pope. His portrait occupied the last vacant place in St Paul's Basilica in Rome addressed to the Popes. Francis Jorge Mario Bergoglio was the Jesuit who displaced the previous Pope Benedict, Joseph Ratzinger. The Jesuits were to be the main link between the Catholic Church and the Lords.

A fairy tale? But at that time I was a part of this conspiracy, it seemed to me not just a fairy tale and a conspiracy theory, but a hellish plan. And what does God say to all this? He looks calmly and says: "Find yourselves. I have given you a power that you do not know how to use. It's not where you are, what you have, but who you are."

18

It was bubbling, boiling, trembling inside me. If I didn't have Beti by my side, I would explode. So many things piled up in my head, so many different things that mixed together and created a very explosive mix. Optimism and pessimism were handing each other the doorknob to my rooms. The day was pleasant, but the nights when Beti slept were unbearable. All the demons of the world were coming inside me and beseeched me:

"Kill yourself. If not, we will kill you. Slowly, we will mangle you and crush you to the end. You are trying in vain. We always win."

One day, when I asked Beti where we were going on a trip, she said:

"Let's go to the Višarje."

"What are we going to do there?"

"I see you need peace; maybe you can find it there."

I was surprised by her answer. We went to Višarje. We parked the car in the car park of the cable car station in Treviso in Italy and set off, on foot, towards Višarje. We talked a little. In silence, each of us with our own thoughts, we climbed the hill. First, I was looking for the meaning of this journey. Soon I felt that the path was comfortable, that it was calming. I didn't think about anything, I just focused on my step. Left, right, left, right. The second half of the way I felt even more peace and the beauty of the nature around us. Peace, peace, how I missed you. Then I started thinking about the cataclysm that was hanging over our heads. I fought. Good fought evil, light fought darkness, I fought masters. Was it the destination that matters, or was it the journey? There are different paths to get to your destination, but only one is the right one. You can get your money honestly or by deceit. You can buy a car, or you can steal one. You live until you die being honest with yourself, honest with other people and honest with the universe, or you cheat everyone and yourself most of all. You can do nothing. Are you still a human being, or are you just a tree trunk? Should I live as if nothing has happened and nothing will happen? Or should I join my masters and betray Joseph and friends to atone for my sins against them and go on living as their slave. Should I fight until the end of my life, and when I die I will have a smile on my mouth because I will have left the world where I tried to live honestly, perfected? What is fair? The answer was clear, clearer than ever before when I wondered what to do.

We rested at the top, then Beti went to the church. I stayed outside and sat down in the grass. I calmed my breathing and my heartbeat. I was staring at grass that was different in size and shape from its sisters. I have been there and I have not been there. I've been everywhere. I have flown around the world, around the solar system, around the galaxy, around the universe, around the universes. I felt the universe; I felt the force that created it. I was part of that force. My rapture was interrupted by Beti. We left. We left the hill, which brought me some much-needed peace.

We talked all the way down. We didn't draw the future, we promised to be together until the end. She told me:

"It's right that we chose this path. You have changed. There is still sadness in your eyes, but you have accepted it. It is no longer lording over you, and you have overcome anger, rage and fury. I see you, David."

I squeezed her to me. She came to me as a wall creeper, we were one. We were a mighty tree, defying all storms. On the way home, we stopped for a while in Kranjska Gora. Dinner, a walk of two lovers. That night we made love like never before. She was mine, I was hers.

The date of our departure for Mexico was approaching. Beti was looking forward to the journey; I was looking forward to her childish joy. I have talked a lot with my mother in the last few days. She knew something was going on inside me, but she didn't ask me what was weighing me down. My mother seemed old, sick and tired. Her eyes were still sparkling, but her complexion was ashen, her hair thin, her step slower, her voice softer.

"What's wrong with you, Mum?"

"What's going on, I'm getting old. In four years, I'll be seventy," she said, with a forced smile. "Don't worry about me. You'd better take care of yourself, because you're not exactly a flower either. Life is not just sex n' drugs n' rock n' roll," she sang, looking me in the eye.

I smiled and, after a long time, hugged her and squeezed her tightly. I felt a vague fear that I would lose her, that she would leave and I would be alone. She was warm, soft. It seemed to me that her body was fading away. My tears began to drip down on her shoulders. She too was silent. We cried, mother and son.

She didn't want to tell me anything, she was hiding something. Maybe she'll tell me when I get back from Mexico, I thought. I hoped that I was imagining all this because I was always under the influence of negative forces and an uncertain future, and that everything was fine with my mother. Ah these voices; were they real or just an echo of the struggles raging inside me, I wondered. I would like to take her with me to Mexico. I cared about her.

19

We arrived in Tulum on the evening of the 23rd of October, after many changes and waiting at airports. Brian and Karen were already there. They rented a nice seaside house with a large terrace. We were on holiday again. The next day, we were joined by Vasili and black-haired Katarina, his new companion. Diving, laughter, wine, great food. Dalmatia revisited. First, we planned that just me and Brian meet Kamala and Joseph. We needed their willingness and consent to introduce them to Dr Thomas Kendall and the ex-spy, Vasili. On the evening of the 25th, Vasili quarrelled with the locals. He was drunk and his fists itched. Brian and I reacted quickly and dragged him away from the hot-blooded men to avoid a fight. It could have been disastrous for him, and we would have had to get involved. And finally, the police. We absolutely could not allow that to happen. This would seriously jeopardise our mission in Tulum. We escorted Vasili to his room and locked him in. The next morning, he apologised and said:

"Next time, shoot me like a scabby dog."

"I believe that will never happen again," I said.

"I promise it won't," he said, crossing himself and kissing a large gold cross sprinkled with coloured stones, which he wore on a thick gold chain around his neck.

At five o'clock, we knocked at the address the McCormacks had given us. Kamala opened the door and invited us into a large air-conditioned lounge. Joseph was waiting for us there.

"Hello, how have you been travelling?" he greeted us, and led us through the lounge to the spacious garden, which was well protected and guarded on all sides. The extra caution that Vasili advised us to take dictated that I took a good look at the table and chairs and the surroundings. I was hoping that there were no microphones installed anywhere. I found nothing, but I said, anyway:

"We travelled well, bringing along our partners who joined us on holiday in Tulum. We want to invite you to dinner, but our friends have decided not to join us. What do you say; would you like to have dinner with us?"

Joseph and Kamala immediately understood the invitation:

"We are happy to join you. May I suggest a restaurant, or do you have any suggestions?" replied Joseph.

"We are happy to accept your proposal," said Brian.

We each drove two kilometres south from their house in our own car. On the white sand by the sea, there were tables set well apart from each other, so we could talk without interruption. In addition, the voices were drowned out by the waves of the Caribbean Sea.

"How are you?" I asked them when we ordered dinner and had an aperitif.

"Thank God we are very good, in fact, we are excellent. Our work is progressing well, so we are confident that in January we will have the first batch of our nano-robots, which will be programmed to destroy all other foreign substances in the body and also to look after the health of individual cells. What's more, as we told you in Whistler, these nano-robots look after themselves and their reproduction. They are virtually indestructible and can outlive humans, or die with them."

"Excellent," I continued. Then we told them about our visit to Tofino and the arrangement with Dr Kendall.

"Wonderful," said Joseph. "With such people, the chances of ultimate success are even greater. Do you think it would be possible to meet him?"

"Of course," I replied. "Dr Kendall is already here in Tulum. We didn't want to introduce him before we had both agreed to meet him. Our work must go on uninterrupted, no matter what happens to any of us."

"That is why Dr Al-Abadi and his wife are here with us in Tulum. A long-time friend and colleague in whom we have complete confidence. We also wanted to introduce him to you. He will replace us in case anything happens to us that could hinder or even stop the project."

"Very good," Brian spoke up. "Our friend, Vasili, came with us as our future reserve, or substitute, and we trust him completely."

"I don't see any problems. The day after tomorrow, I propose that we all board a small boat and go to sea. The owner and captain of the boat is an old friend of ours. We will be able to spend the day together in the middle of the sea, talking in peace and safety. Be at the yacht harbour at 9 am. The ship is an old wooden barge and can be seen from a distance. You can't miss it. Otherwise, we'll be there, together with Dr Al-Abadi and his wife."

"Deal," I said. "Tomorrow we'll visit Dr Kendall and talk to him."

After dinner, Brian and I drove to our home in Tulum. Vasili sat alone on the terrace, lemonade in hand.

"How was it, boys?"

"Excellent," I replied. "In two days, we are going to the sea together to get to know each other and discuss how we will work in the future."

Then we explained everything to him until the women joined us.

The next day, Brian and I went to the Hotel Maria del Mar in the morning. At the reception, we asked for Dr Kendall. We were kindly told that he was waiting for us at the hotel pool bar. We saw Dr Kendall from a distance. We joined him. He suggested we take a walk by the sea, where we can talk without disturbance.

We told Dr Kendall about our meeting with the McCormacks and passed on their desire to get everyone together on the boat, where we can get to know each other better and discuss. The doctor accepted the invitation and said:

"This case has changed my life completely. From a pleasant and peaceful monotony, I'm full of adrenaline again. During this time I visited my friends who are on the list and told them everything I know about the nano-conspiracy. They are all ready to receive and distribute vaccines. So no prior discussions with them are necessary. What's more, you will deliver these vaccines to my friend at Pfizer, who will then distribute them around the world, where my friends will accept them and arrange for their distribution to vaccination centres in each country. We have a fully prepared infrastructure for vaccinating people. I can be there when vaccines are delivered to Pfizer to make sure there are no complications."

"Excellent, Dr Kendall," I said. "Mr McCormack assures us that the vaccine will be available in January next year. The vaccine contains programmed nano-robots that will take care of their own reproduction in the human body. Their task will be destroying other nano-robots and repairing and replacing the defective cells with new cells built by these robots. In fact, they will look after human health."

"This is very good news indeed. This can help us overcome or at least slow down the Earth Depopulation Project. But we should not be lulled into complacency by these successes. Sarrah, my friend from Seattle, is well informed about everything and can at any time take over my role. I fly once a week from Victoria on a scheduled flight with seaplane to Seattle, so I keep her up to date with everything that's going on. Many times I've flown to Seattle before, at least twice a month, so now I'm not suspicious about doing so."

"Tomorrow, when we all meet together, we will agree on the next steps," said Brian. "If anything happens to David and me so that we can't contact and work with you, we will be replaced by our friend Vasili, whom we will present to you tomorrow. The McCormacks also have a replacement for themselves, who will also be presented tomorrow. Together, we have made sure that work must, in any case, continue, uninterrupted, because if our chain is broken, the world will perish."

We talked for a while, then Brian and I said goodbye and went back to the girls and Vasili. We reported to him about the meeting with Dr Kendall. After our meeting with the doctor, I was in a very good mood. I wanted to be with Beti, so I devoted the rest of the day to her. We rented a boat and went snorkelling on the coral reef. We also had the evening to ourselves. After a delicious dinner, we indulged ourselves to the Caribbean rhythms that lured us onto the dance floor. Beti immeasurably enjoyed it. I enjoyed it because she was right there with me. But when I think about it, Beti has always been a part of me, except that I never admitted it to myself. Maybe now my subconscious has made me do it, when I have become part of a conspiratorial team that will stand up to the masters of the world, that I am opened up to Beti and showed my affection for her. I don't know what would happen to me, if I hadn't had her by my side in those moments. The ordeals that have befallen me have left an impact on my psyche. Beti cushioned them. But despite this, I started to feel the effects of the pressures I have been under recently. In addition to worse sleep, my stomach was also rumbling. My mother was also on my mind. I was on the rack whether to call her or not. My mother was a dark spot in the emerald Tulum.

20

Fifteen minutes before nine, we were already in port. The barge was at the beginning of moorings and visible from afar, because it stood out from the other super modern yachts. The McCormacks and a balding older gentleman of smaller stature were already on board; next to him was a pleasant lady of middle age and darker complexion, with a light shawl around her head. Al-Abadi's. Not far from the boat, Dr Kendall was walking up and down the quay. We boarded the boat together. There was a get-to-know-you session and we set sail shortly afterwards. The captain was a black-haired elderly Mexican man, who from afar looked like a real sea wolf. He was helped by his two sons in their late thirties.

We agreed to talk in small groups because there were too many of us to talk together. Me and Brian, Karen and Beti, Vasili and Katarina, Dr Kendall, both McCormacks and Al-Abadis. I and Brian were the moderators and we made sure that the information circulated and we also dictated the topics we discussed. Each of us knew exactly what our role was. Joseph was extremely pleased with the meeting. He was particularly fascinated by Dr Kendall. The Al-Abadis were also pleasant interlocutors. They were calmer. One could even say that they acted as two spiritual authorities. Vasili was in charge of entertainment and safety. He had seen it all, heard it all. Immediately after setting sail, before we even started, he inspected the boat and spoke to the captain. It was all fine.

Brian and I spoke to the McCormacks before we landed in Las Uvas on the island of Cozumel. Karen and Beti were with us.

"Very interesting people," said Joseph. "With a team like this, we can throw the Earth off its courses, which is what we will in fact do. We will do our utmost to ensure that in the second half of January we start distributing the vaccine with our nanorobots. I therefore propose that we get together on 16th of January in Vienna, where Kamala and I will be attending a three-day congress. We hadn't planned to go there, but the date is very convenient for our final arrangements.

Plus, it's in Europe, close to you, so you won't have to go far to travel. We can meet there at four in the afternoon in the lobby of the Hotel Sacher. In case we can't make it to Vienna, Dr Al-Abadi will be there."

"Right, we'll be there. From my place, where I live, near Kranj in Slovenia, it is about a four hours' drive to Vienna. So that suits me very well, to Brian a little less, because he'll have to fly in from Melbourne," I said, laughing, winked at Brian and said:

"If it was just a meeting in Vienna, then you wouldn't have to come to Europe. But after we meet Joseph and Kamala, we have to go to Canada to see Dr Kendall, so I'd like you to come."

"Of course, I'll come," said Brian. "We have a lot of work to do and a lot of travelling to do. In addition to Kendall, we will also have to visit Monica in Uganda. We will also have to meet Vasili."

"I know, my friend, that we will be together for the rest of our lives, husband and wife," I replied to Brian, without any hesitation.

In Las Uvas, the McCormacks invited us to lunch at a first-class restaurant. "It's in your tourist package," Joseph joked.

We were sitting at a huge table in a secluded area. The McCormacks have proved to be excellent hosts. We all drank the excellent wines recommended by Joseph, only Vasili drank water. He refused to touch alcohol. Accident with locals in Tulum sobered him up. He was aware of his weakness. After lunch, we all took a walk along Uvas beach. Beti and I enjoyed refreshments in the sea. Around five o'clock we sailed back to Tulum, where we said farewell to the McCormacks and the Al-Abadi family. We invited Dr Kendall to join us on our terrace, where we agreed when and where to meet after Vienna. Dr Kendall suggested that we meet his friend Sarah in Seattle, 25th of January. Then he went to his hotel, and we went to spend the rest of the evening on the terrace. Vasili drank two beers, but gave up on the third, when Brian and I told him he could drink as much as he wanted, but we'd tie him up by the table. He smiled sourly, waved his hand and went to the bed.

We stayed together in Tulum for a few more days and had a good taste of the warm Caribbean sun and sea. Beti and I were always together. It was our last holiday. I didn't know that at the time. Vasili and Katarina left us first. We agreed with Vasili that he would come to Vienna on the 16th of January. After two days, we left too, Brian and Karen flew to Australia with a stopover in Argentina to visit friends, while Beti and I flew straight home. I was worried about my mother.

21

It was a long journey home. Originally, we would have flown directly from Cancun to Frankfurt. But there was a mix-up and we flew first to Atlanta and from there to London, where we had the best connection to Ljubljana, so we didn't have to wait too long. But the flight from Atlanta was delayed, so we had to stay overnight in London. We flew to Ljubljana the following afternoon. Many times I called my mother. First from Cancun, then from Atlanta and also from London. But I couldn't get her.

When we got home, my mother wasn't at home. Her car was in the garage, she wasn't there. I asked my neighbour if she might know where she was. She told me that my mother was taken by ambulance to the emergency room in Ljubljana. I made enquiries at the emergency room about what was wrong with her. But they couldn't help me because they don't forward information on the phone. I had to wait until the next day and go in person to the Ljubljana Clinical Centre. After a long wait and a lot of enquiries, I was only told she was taken to the Oncology Institute. There again, the enquiry. Fortunately, I met a doctor who examined my mother when she was brought there.

"I'm sorry to tell you that your mother is very ill. Did you perhaps observe anything unusual in her so far, because she did not want to say what problems she was having until she collapsed and had to be rescued by ambulance and transported to the emergency room? From there, they sent her to us."

"No, I noticed changes in her before I went to Mexico, but she denied that there was anything wrong with her. So it's cancer?" I asked, fearfully.

"Unfortunately, she has pancreatic cancer, which is very advanced. Practically there is nothing more we can do. We can only ease her pain."

"How much time does she have left?"

"Unfortunately, we don't know, but the prognosis is not good. Her life can end very quickly."

"You mean this year?"

"Anything I tell you would be inaccurate and redundant."

"I understand. When can I see her?"

"Tomorrow."

"Can she come home? My partner and I will look after her."

"We can arrange for her to be at home. At home care will help you with a patronage service."

When I returned home, Beti was with her family. That was a big blow for me. Father died when I was a little boy. And now my mother. Why she kept her problems in silence from me, why she didn't tell me. That was my mother. She didn't let me get into trouble with her and her problems. She took care of my upbringing and education, then she didn't interfere in my life anymore. She didn't want me to deal with hers. She lived her life. She enjoyed life. I hoped it would last. I took her picture and burst into tears. How cruel life is, how cruel the departure of a dear one. What is death? Is this the end of everything, or the beginning of something new? Death, death, death. Your eternal unknown. Do we really live only to die one day? What is the point of this? What's the point of chasing success all your life, chasing the devil's money, reproduction, eating, drinking? What is the point of having a mind that eventually dies with us? There is no point. It would be best to die, to sleep into eternity. Sleep. Posthumous life? There is no evidence for it, you can only believe in it. You can only believe that when you come to the end of the road and crash into the wall that separates this world from the next, that there is life beyond the wall, in heaven or in hell. You can believe in eternity, but the mind and science resist. I would like my mother and I to meet there, beyond the wall, but that is wishful thinking that will never be confirmed in this world. I decided to stay with my mother until the end. I would not go to Vienna. I hoped that she would live for a while without suffering. I was prepared to help her in her last days. I wanted to be there for her, to hold her hand when she would leave.

The next day, Beti and I went to Ljubljana to see my mother. When we walked through the door in her sick room, her brown eyes lit up on her fallen face.

"David."

I walked over and hugged her. Tears welled up in my eyes. "Mum. My mother, why didn't you tell me?"

"What should I tell you? I didn't feel well. Now and then something pricked me, but I thought it was part of the aging that was knocking at my door. I didn't know it's that bad."

"I spoke to the doctor. You can go home. Beti and I will take care of you."

"Don't worry about it. I don't want to be a burden on you."

"It's not a burden for me, Mum. I want to take care of you. This is the most important thing for me right now."

"Are you sure you'll be able to look after a sick old lady who can't even go to the toilet on her own?"

"Mum, I can do it all. Don't worry," I said, smiling at her.

Two days later, my Stanka came home. We quickly turned her room into a sick room with a sick bed and everything we needed to take care of the patient. All my adult life I have spent wandering around the world, with a thousand things on my mind, and now, in my mind, it was just my mother. I hadn't even considered the nano-apocalypse. After one week, my mother was up and taking care of herself alone. If she had enough strength, we would always talk. She told me about my father, whom I didn't know. He died when I was not yet two years of age. Ironically, he died of pancreatic cancer.

"Egon, your father, was a great man. The few years we spent together was the best time of my life. In his short life, he has not known defeats; there were no obstacles for him. He always said so be it as God wills, though he wasn't religious. People loved him. He was my great love. Our common life was poetry. Then you came, it was perfect. For a year and a half, we were together, then Egon fell ill. Within two months, he became completely weak and died. For me, this was the hardest period. I was left alone with you, without my love, without my husband.
It was difficult, but I had you. You are unique, but in many ways you are like your father. I was your mother, but I also wanted to be your friend."

"Mum, you're my best friend."

"I hope I was. I didn't want to raise you according to my own or society's norms. I wanted your spirit to be free. We had democracy. I never did things you didn't like. But I also did not let it come to anarchy. I hope I have succeeded. What do you say?"

"Of course you have succeeded; everything that is good in me is yours. I don't know what my path would have been without you. I am grateful for your liberal outlook on life. I have never abused the freedom you gave me. Well, almost never," I said, and smiled.

"We have all done it. That's when we are at our wisest and we don't let anyone give us advice. If I had to walk with you once more from childhood to adolescence, I would not change anything. Do you agree?"

"I agree, Mum. I am very grateful for all you have done for me. You never bothered me: 'you have to be home at ten because you get up at six in the morning'. I remember when I came home in the middle of the night and went to school in the morning. You didn't say anything, just smiled when I struggled to get up and wandered around the flat before I came to. I needed at least seven hours of sleep, so I no longer allowed myself to cut my sleep short. But if it did happen, I didn't go to the school the next day and you were understanding. That's why it never occurred to me to abuse your trust, understanding and open-mindedness."

"That's called responsibility. That's what I've always tried to do. Every human being must set his own boundaries. If others put them on you, then you are limited, a closed bird in a cage, and an animal creature in a zoo. Some of us just can't stand it that others shape our lives, although, unfortunately, there is no such thing as total freedom in this world. But some are servants and need a master over them. I don't condemn them, but I have never allowed their views to influence me in any way. Egon was like that. He respected the social norms and conditions of the time, but he lived in his own way. That's why we were made for each other. The six years that we spent together, it was real life. We never bothered each other's life with the conditions in society at the time. We lived our lives in circumstances that were available to us at that time and we were living in that particular moment, in the time that was intended. When you live your life, it doesn't matter when or where you live. It is important how you live. It doesn't matter how much money you have on your account, or how many different juices or yoghurts are on the shelves in shops. You simply live, you breathe at the top of your lungs. That's the way we people are, that's why they say you get used to everything. Even to death. Not all, but some."

"I don't want to talk about death."

"Why not? Death is a part of life. It is one of the most reliable things that happens to us in our existence in this world. Why should we fear it if we know it is inevitable? It is better to live with it and be prepared for it. I am aware of the transience, but I live and breathe, even now as we speak. And I am increasingly convinced that death is not the end. I look forward to meeting Egon again. I am not religious, but what I am, what we all are, cannot die. It is alive; it is part of the spiritual universe. I don't know where the beginning is and where the end is, but I do know that this life and this world we live in is just a tiny piece of an atom compared to the universe. Awareness is not made up of atoms, but much more. It is part of the energy that created space. Sorry, David, for being philosophical and bothering you with my esoteric reflections."

"I don't forgive you," I said, and laughed. "I'm happy to listen to you. We've never talked about that before."

"There was no opportunity. Everything in this world has to come of age. So that this conversation has also matured. I have matured and now I am going, you are still maturing."

She took my hands, looked me in the eyes and said in a difficult voice:

"Don't be afraid of me. I'm moving on to a better place, and you're staying in this uncertain world. I shall fear for you."

She was getting more and more tired. I sat next to her in silence, then she fell asleep. This was our last lengthy conversation. After that day, she could no longer muster enough strength, to be able to talk for so long.

22

The time of farewell was approaching. There were days when she didn't say a word. But then came the days when she got the power to speak from I don't know where. One of the last, it was mid-December, when she said to me:

"Before I go, tell me what's wrong with you. I know there is something going on inside you and I want you to tell me before I die. I'm not forcing you, but maybe it will be easier if you tell me."

I told her everything. I thought it was right to tell her. Her understanding and her perception of the world has accepted the kind of stories of which I have been a part. Her words are etched in my memory.

"There are no coincidences and you were chosen for a reason. The universe, or the almighty Creator Himself, has chosen you. Whether you will succeed, I don't know. But know that I am proud of you for doing right. That's all that counts, the path you walk. The journey is more important than the destination. The aim is not sanctifying the means, but on the contrary, the means sanctify the end. The goal is not death, but what follows death."

Then it got worse and worse for her. She never got out of bed again. Morphine was her last companion. Beti and I were always by her side. I couldn't have done it without her. Mother's last words were:

"I am not afraid to die."

I was shaken by her farewell, and even now, as I write this, tears are welling up in my eyes. The day before she died, she was breathing heavily, writhing in pain, and apparently the morphine had no more help. I told her:

"Mum, today is my birthday."

She heard me and lifted her body a few millimetres and pursed her lips. I kissed her. The last kiss. She slept soundly that night. I stayed up all night next to her. In the morning, I was replaced by Beti. Beti was religious, so she prayed with her while she combed mother's hair. It started around midday. Her breathing became more and more laboured. We were right next to her. I held both her hands and kept her calm. She was gasping for air. I knew it was death that had entered her room. Shortly before she died, a nurse arrived. She had nothing more to do. Mum's last struggle; she just watched silently. When my mother stopped breathing, I screamed:

"She died."

Beti and I cried. After a minute or so, my mother started breathing again. Sister came to me and took me to the door and said:

"Please don't cry. She came back because she was afraid you wouldn't let her go. Allow her to leave."

I went back to my mother, who was still breathing. With tears in my eyes, I told her:

"Come on, Mum. Everything will be fine with me and Beti. Go on, don't worry about me."

Then she left, for good.

Brian and Karen also came to the funeral. We buried her without pomp, with a priest.

When she could still joke, she said:

"If you don't mind, you can give me a church burial. It can't do any harm."

I fulfilled her wish. When her coffin was lowered into the ground, I looked up at the sky and said to myself:

"Goodbye Mum, say hello to Dad. See you up there one day."

Brian and Karen stayed in Slovenia until we left for Vienna. They wanted to stay in a hotel, but I wanted them with me and Beti. It was easier for me if there were more of us in the house, but she was missing. My Stanka was missing. She ended her life as the universe intended for her. Now as I write this, my opinion has changed. She said goodbye at the right time. She was spared the uncertainty and torment of awaiting her death sentence.

23

We left for Vienna in the early morning of the 14th of January. Brian was at the helm, with me next to him, Karen and Beti behind. Brian and I didn't talk much while the two women chatted. We planned our route via Klagenfurt to Vienna. We drove calmly along country roads. We were in no hurry. We stopped in Knittelfeld and had lunch. During lunch, Brian called Vasili, who reported that he had been involved in a very severe car accident and had suffered serious injuries. He would be in the hospital, where he had undergone a number of operations, for at least three more months, and then a long recovery. In practice, he was not operational for at least half a year. This meant trouble for us, because we were seriously counting on him to help us and replace us when needed. We decided to make our way to Vienna together, but we would work and travel separately after this Vienna trip. After meeting the McCormacks, Brian would go to Canada and I would go to Copenhagen, where I would meet my friend, Marghrete, and try to arrange for her to help us perhaps. If I could do it, then we would go to Canada together, assuming, of course, that Marghrete could join me. There, I would introduce her to Brian and Dr Kendall, later also Joseph and Kamala. We have temporarily solved an unexpected problem. Now, just before we get the vaccines, it was necessary to be operational and well organised. I knew Marghrete and I was sure she could help us. We continued our journey towards Vienna. Just outside Vienna, there was a motorway traffic accident. We were a few cars behind the accident. The road was completely blocked. We were stuck and hoped that the traffic would clear as quickly as possible. Unfortunately, that did not happen. There was a long queue of cars. For twelve hours, we were dependent on the help of people who brought us water and food. The biggest problem was the need for toilets. We arrived in Vienna early the next morning.

    We rested all day in rooms at the Opera Suites Hotel, in the vicinity to the hotel Sacher, where we were to meet the McCormacks the following day. In the evening, we went to the city and had dinner in one of the restaurants. On the way back on foot to our hotel, we met a group of hooligans who attacked an elderly couple and wanted to rob them. Brian and I came to the aid of the attacked couple and helped them together. We rescued the couple, but we took it away with minor injuries. They were making my face ugly and making it impossible for Brian to walk normally. Back at the hotel, we sat at the bar and talked about the adventures of the journey and the city.

"I'm slowly becoming superstitious," I started the conversation. "Vasili's accident, the accident before Vienna and our twelve-hour wait on the motorway, and then this. I hope that these events are not portents of something bad."

"The events are not linked," Brian continued. "I think it's just a matter of coincidence that so many things have happened to us in such a short space of time."

"Interesting coincidences," Karen said.

"But we came out of all those accidents as winners, didn't we?" said Beti.

"It's true. I may be influenced by these events, but a certain negativity, or rather, fear, crept in. I fear tomorrow, even though I have no reason to be afraid, except for these peripheries that have spiced up this journey. I just don't know."

"David, my dear friend, you can certainly put it down to that fight, which we took part in and that twelve-hour torment in the cold in the car. Your mind is under the impression of these events, and now, based on these sends false signals that this is not all yet. These suggestions are made by your brain, not some supernatural forces looking after us somewhere in another dimension. Tomorrow everything will be fine once you've had a good night's sleep and we meet with Kamala and Joseph, you'll see," Brian reassured me.

But my mind, or the spirit above us, or whoever, was right, unfortunately for us. Our work, our hope, our hope for the world, was instantly dashed, frozen, dissolved. Brian and I arrived at the Hotel Sacher, half an hour before the appointed time. We sat in the armchairs in the lobby and watched the people who were there at the time. McCormacks usually arrive before the appointed time, but this time they were not there. We waited and they were not there, nor was Dr Al-Abadi, who would have had to replace them if they had not been able to come. We waited nervously for four hours, but nothing happened. The alarms started to sound.

"What are we going to do?" asked Brian.

"I have no idea. We have not made sufficient and well-thought-out provision for back-up plans, which could resolve such hopeless situations. I don't know what prevented them from coming to Vienna. I am surprised that Al-Abadi is not there too."

"This is really strange. We need to provide a communication channel that the intelligence services would not be able to detect and eavesdrop on. We've travelled the globe and met without arranging for a different channel of communication."

"I suggest we come here again tomorrow. Maybe we missed something, maybe we've got something mixed up. We must not give up," I encouraged him and above all, myself.

We changed hotels. Luckily they had rooms available and we moved to the hotel Sacher. We spent the whole day looking out for the McCormacks, and for three more days. Then we were desperate. I left my phone number at the hotel in case they came. Despite the risk, we had no choice. We drove back to Slovenia.

24

When we got home, Brian and I sat down at the computer and immediately started to browse the internet. We took a risk and typed Joseph and Kamala McCormack into the browser. One of the first results was an article in a Californian newspaper that mentioned the violent deaths of the McCormacks and their six friends. It should be an armed robbery that took place just as Joseph and Kamala were hosting their friends. We were shocked. We found a few more articles like this. Finally, we visited the official NASA website, at their Ames Research Centre in Moffett Field, California, where it said that five of their colleagues had died violent deaths. The names Kamala and Joseph McCormack were important to us, as well as Mahmoud Al-Abadi.

"Brian this is a disaster. How could this happen? I don't think it's about a random violent robbery that took place while Joseph and Kamala were at home and hosting their colleagues."

"I'm afraid it's no coincidence. Armed robbery at a time when the house was full? Robbers usually rob when houses are empty, when none of the occupants are home. Somehow they were tracked down."

"I don't know how they got on their trail. Maybe they were betrayed by someone in the team that was supposed to help them with this project. If I remember correctly, Joseph mentioned four friends and colleagues. The dead include three colleagues and both McCormacks."

"Unfortunately, we don't know who the fourth friend is. Is there anything we can do?"

"There is nothing we can do. The nano-robots were in the hands of Joseph and Kamala and their friends. If we embark on a doomed exploration and search for alternatives, they will come for us too. This is a disaster, this is definitely the end."

"You're right, there's no way we can restart this project."

"I suggest we postpone our reflection until tomorrow. Maybe there is just a glimmer of hope."

"On the 25th, we will meet Dr Kendall. All four of us will fly to Canada. Maybe he has a solution."

"Maybe."

I didn't sleep that night. Brian couldn't sleep either. We watched TV for a while, and then we started to think again about the situation that had derailed us and shaken us.

"David, this is a real drama now. We can go on a guerrilla war, but it won't be for long because the mafia will quickly silence us."

"I know. We can advertise that we are looking for nano-scientists." I wanted to be sarcastic.

"We will decide how to proceed after meeting with Dr Kendall. If there are positive forces on our side, then there is a solution. If the universe has also lifted hands, then I go to my ranch in Halls Creek and wait for the end. I will not become a robot and their slave. When it will be so far away, so that there is no way out, I'd rather plant a hawthorn stake in my heart than go on living like a zombie."

"So do I, but where should I retreat?"

"Hey, I have an idea. If it will be necessary to withdraw, then you and Beti will also be able to come to Australia. All four of us will hide in the wilderness. We'll throw away all our electronics and live absolutely primitively. The only link to the world will be my plane, which we will fly to Halls Creek for food and other necessities. I doubt they will be looking for four adventurers who have taken refuge in the wilderness. We will be a nuisance to them and they will let us die behind God's back."

"This is probably the only option that will be acceptable to me. But we will retreat before the borders are closed, which is likely to happen. There is a problem, because Beti and I need a longer visa to stay in Australia."

"David, do you think this is some terribly difficult thing for me to do? Together we will set up a company in Australia to research. I don't know what. We will plan a project that will run for a few years and you will be able to come and go to Australia. And I have a female person who works in the Ministry of the Interior, who owes me a favour."

"It could happen tomorrow, or it could happen in a few years."

"I suggest that if we cannot find a solution, we withdraw immediately to Halls Creek."

"I need to talk to Beti."

"Absolutely."

Then we were silent, but I couldn't be silent for long.

"I knew we were dealing with dangerous stuff, but what happened to Joseph and the others is incomprehensible to me. They were killed without warning. They killed eight people, five scientists. Maybe they are already following us and we will be next on their list for cleaning."

"I doubt it," said Brian. "I think we would be in the next world already if they suspected us. They would not let information spread uncontrolled. The McCormacks were very cautious, so we had no channel of communication other than personal meetings. They were probably also bugged, and as they didn't manage to catch anything except for communication between those killed, a verdict was delivered and swiftly executed."

"I guess that was true. But it is interesting that the execution took place without questioning. They could torture them and then they would come to us."

"I think they started monitoring them and bugging them after our meeting in Mexico. If this had happened in Mexico, we would not be talking now. It is possible that they were followed and controlled shortly after their arrival from Mexico. After two months of constant surveillance, and before McCormack was due to travel to Europe, all those involved were executed, except for a fourth scientist who apparently betrayed them."

"You're right, that's the logic. Apparently, the cautious Joseph was betrayed by a traitor who cost him his life. The various intelligence services are infiltrated into all pores of the society. No one is safe from them. Monica, Dr Kendall and Vasili have proved to be reliable colleagues, or so I hope. From now on, spies will monitor even more what's happening in the world. Whoever says the word 'nano', wherever in the world, alarms will start sounding in intelligence offices. In the era of digital technologies, they can eavesdrop on everyone and monitor every movement of everyone. I suggest we be very careful with mobile phones. Maybe we give up on them completely and get a new appliance with a local phone number wherever we go."

"I agree. We don't need this shit. Beti and Karen are always with us. My parents and I very rarely hear from each other."

I thought of my mother. A burning pain shot through my chest. "She is saved," I said to myself. She is now in a better world than those of us who are still alive. What will our future look like? Whether there is a future at all. Or is it all just an illusion, a nightmare dream? Maybe Mum is in the real world now, together with my father.

"Where did you go?" asked Brian.

"I remembered my mother. She will not experience the shit that is coming into the world. If people know what awaits them, it would be chaos. Suicides, murders, robberies, crimes of all kinds. Maybe it is better that they do not know what's in store for them."

"So you think that if we come out of this shit without a solution, we don't inform the public about the intention of the global elite?"

"I don't know. We can try, but very carefully, because that would expose ourselves too much to the masters. I doubt any result that would suggest that people will take seriously the warning of impending disaster. The elite will do everything to drown this information in a flood of other information and declare them conspiracy theories."

"We will discuss this when it is necessary. Now it's Dr Kendall. The last hope for the planet."

"The last hope; it sounds so apocalyptic and, most shockingly, it really is." A day later, all four of us left for Canada.

25

On the plane on the transatlantic flight, I talked to Beti about the future, which was grey. I told her what options we had after these tragic events, when we lost the main driving force and the only chance of successfully countering the global elite. Beti listened to me with interest.

"I am not afraid of the future as long as we are together," she said.

"My dear, the truth is that there is no future. The world, as we know it, will not exist anymore."

"We will exist as long as we breathe, and that's all that counts for me."

"Brian offered us that when we got to the point of no return, when changes are going to start happening, that we're going to come to him in Australia and we're all going to retreat to his ranch in the wilderness, far from civilization and accessible only by horses, camels or planes."

"I don't know, dear. I have parents and a sister. I don't know how to leave them."

"They can come with us. I will talk to Brian about whether there is a possibility that they can join us."

"I'm ready to go with you to the end of the world, but I don't want to let my loved ones through this terrible period that is coming."

"Maybe it won't be necessary." I hugged her and smiled.

When she fell asleep, I went to see Brian. I asked Karen to sit down with Beti because I had to talk to Brian.

"Beti and I talked about the future. She is ready to come with me to Australia, but worries about her father and mother and her sister. It will be difficult to leave them, she says. I don't want to put her in a position where she has to decide between me and them. She would undoubtedly have chosen me, but such a decision would certainly have marked her and she would no longer be Beti."

"Uh. I hadn't thought of that. Do you have someone who is making it difficult for you to decide to move to Australia?"

"No, I don't. I have aunts, uncles and cousins. But with them I have practically no contacts. If I were to think about them further, this network would grow so large that we would have to hire at least one Airbus A 380."

"OK. So there are three more than you and Beti. Maybe it would work. The more of us there are, the easier it will be to survive. You have made it easier for me to decide about my parents. We'll take them and we'll be together nine."

"Do you think it would work?"

"Of course. We have enough money. In addition to the legacy of Joseph and Kamala, I also have some savings, and my parents are well off."

"I have some savings too beside this money from McCormacks. I will also sell my mother's house. Beti's family is also wealthy because they own their own business. Well, at least it seems to me that they are not in debt, because Beti and I never talked about it."

"Money will not be a problem. When the world reaches its final phase, when everything is under absolute control, we will no longer need the money. We will only depend on ourselves and our hands. Until then, we need to make all the necessary preparations to survive in the wild, out of touch with the outside world."

"Great, I'm going back to Beti to tell her what we agreed."

"David, one small warning. I can arrange the necessary visas, but we must not procrastinate too much. As soon as we decide to go to the ranch, we will have to sort out all the things we need. When the things that will trigger the process of depopulation of the world start to happen in earnest, it will be too late to flee, because it will be impossible."

"I agree."

When I came back to Beti, she was awake and talking to Karen. I didn't want to interrupt, but when they saw me, Karen got up and went to Brian. Travel in the first class allowed us to have an uninterrupted conversation.

"My dear. Tell me your opinion. Would your family be willing to sell everything and come with us to Australia?"

"I don't know. If we tell them everything that is waiting for them, and that if they stay at home, they would have no future and they might lose their lives, then maybe this would convince them. We'll talk to them when we get home."

"Right."

When we landed in Vancouver, we rented a bigger car and drove to Horseshoe Bay, where we boarded a ferry and sailed to Vancouver Island. In

Tofino, we stayed in the same hotel where Brian and I had stayed. Town and the sea were different this time. The greyness did not make us optimistic.

26

"Hello, my friends." Dr Kendall greeted us. "I have so many things to tell you. How did you travel?"

"Hello Dr Kendall. The trip was fine, but everything else is a mess, or rather, chaos, tragedy," I said.

"Let's go out on the terrace." The terrace was glazed and heated. "What happened?"

We told him about the tragic deaths of the McCormacks, Al-Abadi and others. Dr Kendall was silent for a few moments, and then he spoke:

"What a disaster, what a tragedy. I feel sorry for these nice people. So all the effort was in vain. I have practically prepared everything down to the smallest detail so that I could start the vaccine distribution project immediately. Now everything has fallen into disrepair and the world is heading for annihilation. I can't believe it."

"We are of the same mind," said Brian. "We have no idea how to try to re-launch our project. We don't know who we can turn to, that would not endanger ourselves and everyone else."

"There is a way out, but how to find it in this labyrinth, how to find a way where there is no danger. I have to think about everything. Come tomorrow, we'll take the boat out to the sea and talk. Dress well."

"We are not alone in Tofino," I said. "Our girl friends are with us. Can they come along too?"

"Of course, there is plenty of space on the boat. Sarrah is here too. I want you to get to know her. She lives with me, but she is not at home at the moment. Meet me at the harbour tomorrow at 10 am, if that suits you."

"Tomorrow at ten," I repeated. "Don't forget warm clothes."

Brian and I returned to the hotel, where Beti and Karen were waiting for us. The girls of course, agreed for all of us to go to the sea together. After dinner, Beti and I went to our room, Brian and Karen stayed in the hotel bar.

"I was thinking about us all going to Australia together. I hope they will decide to come with us. If they don't go, I'll still be with you, until the end."

"Beti, if it's hard for you to leave your parents and sister, then we'll stay at home too. I have no one else now, except you. If I go to Australia, I will extend my life and nothing else. I don't want you to be unhappy and blame yourself for not staying with them."

"Would you really be willing to do that for me?"

"For you and for us."

She hugged me and started kissing me. We undressed and gave in to the passion that made us completely taken over. I knew her body, but I still discovered something new. Kisses between her breasts or her hips always turned her on so much that she quietly purred like a cat. She also knew how to get me to start to purr like a cat. When I entered her, the world stopped. I looked at her in the eyes and immersed myself in them. We were one. I had to look at her, her face, her body, her breasts, her hips, her legs; I had to watch as I slowly penetrated her. We loved each other. When it came to us, we fell asleep. She was lying on top of me. I miss her, I miss her very much. Now, as I write this, I am reliving our lovemaking, our moments together. I hope to meet you up there, somewhere, soon.

We boarded Dr Kendall's boat at 10 am. Sarrah was a nice white-haired lady in her late seventies. Whether she and Dr Kendall were more than friends was not important. As we slowly made our way out, Dr Kendall spoke:

"Sarrah is my friend and my deputy. Whatever happens to me, she will replace me. She knows everything, so she can carry on where I will finish. Maybe it's not all over yet. I thought for a long time and remembered my friend from my childhood, with whom I am still friends today. He also worked at Ames Research Moffett Field Centre. He is very reliable. First I will check to see if I can talk to him, then I will move on. I don't want to take too many risks, but he is our last resort, at least as far as I am concerned. What do you say?"

"We trust you and your judgement," I replied.

"I won't mention you to him, nor Sarrah. If I see that we can cooperate together, then we will meet. He certainly knows the situation in the Research Centre, and may even have known Joseph and Kamala McCormack personally. They might even have been colleagues. I don't know what his field was, but I don't think he would have a problem getting through to people who have been or are still involved in this project."

"Be very careful," Brian quickly spoke up. "Only mention the word 'nano' once, then replace it with another word. Above all, keep safety in mind, don't use electronic devices."

"Don't worry. I know how these things are done."

After a good two hours of sailing in an otherwise calm sea, we returned to the port. Dr Kendall and Sarrah invited us to lunch in the restaurant well-known to me and Brian. We have agreed to meet again on the first of March in Uganda at Monica's, with the hope that during this time Dr Kendall will find the solution to our problem, to the problem of the whole world.

The next day, the four of us drove to Victoria, where we stayed for three days before we returned home. Brian and Karen flew to Melbourne, we flew to Slovenia. We have agreed to meet together in Entebbe, Uganda, already on the 25th of February. We wanted to show the girls Africa.

"Dude, think about the alternative, about going to Australia," Brian said to me as we said goodbye.

"I think this alternative is the most realistic option, I hope everything will be fine with Kendall. I doubt very much that he would be able to connect us to a reliable link that will be able to defy the conspiracy."

"Hope dies last, they say. *Vaya con Dios amigos.*"

"*Vaya con Dios.* Take care of yourselves."

"You too."

There was hope, but I was quite firmly convinced that there was very little hope. I did not want to burden others with my opinion.

27

We returned home to my mother's house. The journey to Vienna, the death of the McCormacks and our trip to Canada took me some distance from my mother. But an empty house at home reminded me that my mother was gone. No more of her laughter, her eye-rolling, her measured words. The wound has reopened. I was grieving for my mother, the only person who really knew me. Why illness and then death? Do we live only to die? At the beginning, at the end or in between. I missed her and I still miss her today. As long as she was alive, it was a given that she was at home and I was wandering around the world. I didn't miss her then because I knew she was home. She was gone, I missed her. We do not know how to appreciate the life we have and the people who are with us until they are gone forever. Thank God that Beti was by my side. This gentle and unpretentious soul, whose reason for living was love and surrender. Apart from the loss of my mother, I was also plunged into melancholy by this ominous future that would become completely real because there was no more Joseph and Kamala, who bravely defied it. To live as a slave or to die, that was now the question. No, this was not a dilemma at all. Live freely and die freely, because death comes in anyway. Why do we cling to this miserable life when we know that it will end one day somewhere? We cling to life because love holds us up.

Sorry Pero. Love. What is love? Is it a one plus one, is it a big chocolate with hazelnuts, is it youthful kissing, crazy sex, holding hands? It's probably love for everything that creates and gives meaning to life. Love is the world, it is the universe, and it is the force that created the Universe? We are really stupid people. The universe gives us life and love, and we ourselves create hatred. Why? Because we are afraid of love, because we are afraid of creation, because we are afraid of ourselves and our power? My mother gave me love, Beti gave it to me. What about me?

Beti and I talked a lot about the future. What future awaits us? When will it happen, when will it burst, when will the countdown begin. Beti made a conscious decision to go to Australia anyway, with or without her parents. She wanted to live free; she wanted to live with me.

"Let's take the time we have left," she said.

We took it and went. But maybe it wouldn't be necessary to flee to Australia. Maybe the Creator was on our side. Maybe Dr Kendall would find a solution and we will save the world. I wanted to believe in it, but somehow it didn't work. Not that the faith was weak, but here the mind was in the advantage that has judged that there is very little chance of resolving the situation. Nevertheless, there was a modicum of faith left, a nano-smidgen. Uganda would seal our fate.

We spent most of our time at home, next to each other, with each other, in each other. We took daily walks in the nearby fields and forests. This was around Trstenik. We used to take her parents' dog with us. How true it is that everyone sees the world according to his own mood. This time were the forests and meadows melancholic, just like me. But love holds us up. Beti was as aware of the uncertainty as I was, but she saw the meaning of life in me. I loved her, I admired her, but unfortunately, my purpose was not only her. I wanted a world where we will live, the world as it was before.

"It's time to talk to my family," she said.

"Yes. Let's go and see them tonight, or better, invite them to dinner."

"Right. Today is Wednesday, I suggest we invite them on Saturday when they are free."

"Accepted. What do you think? Will they accept this apocalyptic future as fact or as a conspiracy theory of mentally ill fanatics?"

"It will be strange at first, but when we tell them everything, I think they will understand. The question is whether they will decide to sell everything up, leave everything behind and move to Australia. Especially given that there are no set timeframes for when this should happen."

"If it is your decision to come with me to Australia in any case, then I suggest, in case of a debacle in Uganda, that we travel later this year and let's organise our life there. And your family can come after us any time, as long as it's possible."

"I agree with you. Once this deadly virus emerges, all travel will be impossible very quickly, so it's a good idea to leave earlier."

"As long as we don't limit ourselves to the ranch and Halls Creek, we can explore Australia and learn how to live and survive in its wilderness. Brian and Karen will definitely be good mentors."

"Aside from what lies ahead, I'm looking forward to going and living there."

"How do you feel about our project? Will we continue or will it be over?"

"If I say what I think and what I know, then the chances of survival after the death of your friends are very small. The world will change, people will die."

"Unfortunately, I have a similar opinion. But let's not be too pessimistic, perhaps in the cradle of humanity, a new hope for its survival will be born."

"My prayers are always for this hope."

Then we returned home. We made a plan on how we would deal with her parents and a sister. Everything else was of secondary importance. Convincing her family to join us. That would mean a lot to Beti. It would be easier for me too, because she would be satisfied.

28

Beti and I prepared dinner together. The last supper, because after this supper, nothing would be the same. Her parents were quite wealthy. They founded and managed their own company for the production of electronic components for the automotive industry, which became an important partner for all major European automotive concerns. The company also employed their two daughters, the younger, Beti, and the older, Klara, who would take over the company when Rudi and Ana retired. Klara was married, but her husband died in a car accident a few years ago. They didn't have any children, so Klara gave herself completely to the company. Beti was the opposite. Klara was stricter with herself and her surroundings, focused only on her work without private life, without any desire to live a different life than the one she had lived. While Beti was in love with life, in love with life with me. Klara was like this even before her husband died. They probably didn't decide to have children because children would have gotten in the way of their work. Her husband also worked in the family business. He died on a business trip on his way back from Stuttgart.

Ana and Rudi were equally serious, strict and hard-working, but they knew how to enjoy life. Every year, they enjoyed a caravan seaside holiday in the summer, a skiing holiday in the winter, and occasionally a longer trip, especially since their daughters grew up and they were able to run the business without them. They were in their sixties, just as my mother was. We were neighbours, so to speak, with only a few houses between us.

After a Mediterranean dinner with a wide variety of fish and other wonders from the Adriatic Sea, we sat down in the lounge, each of us with our own glass of wine in hand. I lit a fire in the fireplace to create a cosy atmosphere. I told them to leave their mobile phones at home that evening, because Beti and I wanted the evening just for us.

"We have invited you here today for a purpose," I began. "In April and May last year, I spent some time in Geneva, reporting from CERN. On my first day there, I was invited to join two scientists, a husband and wife, who were working on a very important project funded by major global organisations and corporations. They presented me with a secret project that would completely change the lives of the entire population of the world in a positive way. Unfortunately, it turned out that the decision-makers had completely different intentions with this project. Instead of improving the quality of life of the world's population, a life free from hunger and disease, and with the possibility of survival for a much larger number of people than the current world population is, the decision-makers decided to use the project for their own goals, which were the exact opposite of the goals of improving people's lives. Their satanic goal was to depopulate the world with various diseases that would lead to many deaths, enslavement and control of the survivors who would be their chosen ones. The world's population is set to fall to five hundred million people."

"Hey, hey David, stop it," Rudi interrupted my speech. "Are you serious or are you just trying to make or break our evening with fables?"

"Dad, David is completely serious," said Beti.

Rudi shrugged his shoulders and, with a strange expression on his face, as if he had experienced something unexpected, unimaginable, something sinister, he collapsed back into his armchair. Anna showed no emotion or strange signs of being disturbed by my story. Klara, on the other hand, found my story completely nonsensical, gibberish and far-fetched, which she clearly confirmed with her facial expressions.

"What are you trying to tell us with all this journalistic bullshit?" said Klara, with a hint of contempt in her voice.

Beti spoke again:

"Do you think David is telling you fairy tales, that's why we called you here, to shake nonsense and infantile fabrications on your head? I believed him immediately. Our recent travels together have confirmed what I believed. I met the world's top experts who spoke very seriously about the ominous future for humanity."

The words spoken by Beti were effective. All three of them have since listened to my stories with more or less genuine interest, or so it seemed to me.

"The original intention of the two scientists who intercepted me in Geneva was to send information to the world through me about a worldwide conspiracy and the total destruction of man as we know him. While we were still in Switzerland, we had the idea that maybe we could save the world, or postpone its transformation for a longer period of time. With the help of science and its achievements, or with the same weapons that the conspirators wanted to subjugate the world to themselves, this madness could be stopped, at least temporarily. My friend Brian, who you know, and I managed to organise a small group of reliable people, experts who can make our plan a reality. Unfortunately, everything came to a halt with the death of my friends who I met in Switzerland. Beti and I will be travelling again soon and we will find out if there are any other possibilities for this project, or if it has come to a complete standstill. If the project cannot be implemented, then the black scenario will come true. People will get sick from an artificially created virus that is expected to mutate repeatedly. It will cause mass deaths. The conspirators will try to stop it by vaccinating the population, but to no avail. People will continue to get sick and die as more and more laboratory-perfected viruses circulate. Then, at last, the vaccine that will save the world will arrive. But this vaccine will only save themselves and the five hundred million people they choose to continue living on Earth. They will not be people like us. These will be the new people who will be enslaved by their masters, who will completely influence their thinking. They will work for masters and will no longer be aware of their humanity, human freedom and autonomy."

"How will they make me get vaccinated with their vaccine?" asked Rudi.

"They will gradually force you to do it. First, the vaccinations will be optional. The first vaccine will actually be a vaccine against the virus that causes respiratory diseases. Then more and more sophisticated viruses will start circulating, killing many people. New vaccines will be introduced that are partially successful, and the virus will claim more and more lives. Once the virus has killed off a large part of the world's population, mainly the poor, the sick and the elderly, they will begin to vaccinate the rest of the population with a vaccine containing microscopically small devices at the level of the size of molecules. These devices will definitely protect survivors from the virus. The conspirators, the global elite, the masters, or whatever you want to call them will decide who lives on. These will be the people they need to do different jobs for them. They and their families will be left alive, and the rest will be killed by other deadly diseases caused by these little devices. As well as looking after the survivors and keeping them alive, these mini-devices will also influence the minds and thinking of these people through their masters. They will then be able to control them all the time and show them a world in which they are happy with their lives and have no chance to challenge the rulers. People will essentially be slaves, except they won't realise it and will think they are living in paradise."

Rudi spoke again:

"But if I don't want to be vaccinated, how will they make me?"

"Quite simply, if you are not interesting to them, they will let you die of the virus. But if they are interested, they will force you to lose all your rights, including your property, because you will endanger others by not vaccinating. Then you will be vaccinated or you will die."

"Terrible," said Anna. "I believe you, but it's still so hard to grasp and accept because it's like a script for the craziest sci-fi movie. I don't know what to say."

"Unfortunately, this is a real scenario for the future of the planet. People who knew too much are already dying from it," I said.

"Then why are you telling us this and endangering our lives?" interjected Klara.

"Because I want to save your lives. Because I want you to avoid the chaos that will ensue on Earth."

"How to avoid chaos, are you going to vaccinate us with this vaccine of yours?" asked Rudi.

"If possible, absolutely. In the event that the project ultimately fails, which we will find out very soon, then there is a chance that we will all retreat together, far from everything. Me, Beti, Ana, Klara and you."

"Where can we go?" interrupted Rudi.

"To Australia. Brian has a large estate in the wilderness, far away from everything, accessible only by plane, or by several days of hiking in a very rugged and dangerous landscape. There we can retreat, hide and survive, and decide our own destiny. Away from the world gone mad."

"What should we do with our business, with all the assets we have?" asked Klara.

"My advice is to sell as soon as possible, before the virus breaks out and the crisis hits. Then it will always be a harder sell. In the meantime, we can organize our lives in Australia," I replied.

"I can't believe it," said Rudi. "It's not that simple. How can we just leave everything overnight that we have built all our lives and retreat into the Australian wilderness, behind God's back, waiting for a virus to take us, or animals to eat us, or other diseases to kill us?"

"This is an alternative to what is being planned. Either you will live and die free, or you will survive and die as a slave without mental freedom. The decision is yours. We leave again in a week. If you make a decision before we leave, please let us know, because we can start working on the project already, if necessary of course. You can also tell us your decision after we return home. The sooner you decide, the more time you will have to sell your business and assets and prepare thoroughly for the move." I tried to be neutral. But Beti suggested what they should choose:

"I know it's not easy, but unfortunately it will happen this year, next year, in three years' time, or later. It will happen. We don't know when that will happen. I therefore ask you to think carefully about this. I would like us to live together. If you don't decide to move, I'm definitely going with David."

"We will think about it and let you know," said Ana.

Then they left, there was no atmosphere and no desire to spend the rest of the evening together. Beti and I talked for a long time before falling asleep.

"The problem will be Klara," she said.

29

The night before Beti and I left for Uganda, all three of them came to our house. Rudi started talking before we even sat down:

"So we've decided, we're going to Australia. We will immediately start selling our house, holiday home, cars and boat and other things. We can leave Australia very soon and before we are locked up in a prison on an estate 'in the middle of nowhere', we want to cruise Australia. Klara still has to keep the business this year because it is bound by contracts with customers. In the meantime, she will find a buyer for the company. She plans to join us in Australia next year."

"I have a question," said Klara. "Can my friend and his thirteen-year-old daughter come with me?"

"I don't see any problem," I replied. "We will live in a community of eleven people. There are five of you, me and Beti plus Brian, his girlfriend and his parents. We will talk in more detail when we return from Africa. Maybe we can find a solution there and then relocation won't be necessary, at least not immediately."

The next day, Beti and I travelled to Uganda. Beti was looking forward to going to Africa, while I had mixed feelings. Voices of despair, then of more or less forced hope, were heard inside me. I wanted to stay focused, sober, but the hum of the plane's engines and the sleeping Beti next to me kept bringing me back to a terrible thought: "Hope is over." The search for a solution is a gasping for air that makes us even more tired and exhausted. The predators are patiently waiting to kill us, to prevent our futile attempts to stop them from plundering and finally get rid of us. Is the world we are supposed to know really dying, or is it really being run and subjugated by a group of beings from another planet, another universe? Should I lose my faith and finally give up? Is this life at all? What else can keep me alive? Is that Beti? I love her, but what future do we have? Tarzan and Jane? To fight. For whom? For what? To die. To sleep. To wake up.

I remembered my mother and her dying. She came back to life. Maybe there is hope for life after life. Maybe there is a new life waiting for us after death. But why don't we know that already here in this world, in this life? Is this what the masters are hiding from us, to take away our hope? We work for them; we spend money and health on them, not on ourselves. We don't need Coca-Cola, purple cows, fast food, lots of drugs, expensive parties…to survive. It is all theatre that distracts us from reflecting on our life and its meaning. And we pay for this theatre ourselves, with the crumbs that fall from the master's table. We are blind, deaf and stupid. We roll heavy balls of stone up the hill, but we never reach the top. Finally, we are taken to the slaughterhouse. Religions give us hope, but even that hope is tailored to the masters. They create heaven and hell, and those who believe in it are considered small-minded by non-believers. For those who manage to peer through the veiled windows into spirituality, it is certainly easier. But you don't just get this way in the church, in the mosque, in the temple, where people are told that they must obey their masters and submit to them, or they will not get to heaven. It is up to each individual to find his own way. Is this hope for me?

When we arrived in Entebbe, I managed to shake off the pessimistic thoughts that had accompanied me on the journey. The sunshine and the warm weather put me in an optimistic mood. Brian and Karen had already been to Uganda. We stayed in Kampala for two days, and then went on a two-day cruise on Lake Victoria. On the boat, besides two locals, there were only four of us. Beti and Karen were having their own fun, and I and Brian were talking about the precarious situation.

"I've been thinking a lot about the McCormacks' deaths since we haven't seen each other," said Brian. "I think it will be practically impossible, or very difficult, to find a solution without them. I doubt that Dr Kendall can find a safe way to revive the project."

"I share the same opinion. I'm afraid our only chance of survival is your ranch in the wilderness."

"Yes, it is the only option that gives us partial freedom and, above all, an escape from the chaos that will follow the outbreak of the virus and the resulting pandemic. Karen and I were in Halls Creek. This time I looked at the property in great detail in the light of the permanent settlement there. We have a number of buildings that can be converted into a home, so we don't have to live together. There is also plenty of space for livestock farming and agriculture. There is plenty of water. I have several springs on my property, and they are all close to residential properties. Electricity can be provided by an electricity generator and by solar power. Solar panels can be installed on all building roofs and other sunny locations. There is no shortage of sunshine. We need to make sure we have enough salt, sugar, oil, which we can otherwise produce ourselves, and enough of the other essentials for life. We will also need a fuel tank for the aircraft and for tractors and other agricultural machinery. If there is a move, we need to focus on the detailed planning and implementation of these plans."

"It will be an interesting experience, in a Robinson Crusoe kind of way. Work will dispel the dark clouds that bring storms. Beti's mum and dad could move to Australia as early as this year. The following year, her sister, her partner and his thirteen-year-old daughter. Do you think there will be enough room for everyone?"

"A hundred people can live there, but then different problems arise. It is easier to get along with each other when there are fewer of us. Vasili and one of his partners might even join us. He said he wanted to move to Australia. Before Karen and I return home, we will visit Vasili in Russia."

"Now we're talking as if that's the only option left. Let's wait to hear what Dr Kendall has to say."

"You're right, but the exchange about continuing to live in Australia was not in vain. It will speed up the relocation action, if necessary," Brian concluded our conversation. Then Beti and Karen joined us.

"Everything is easier with you," I said, winking at him.

Those were the last two days of our lives when there was still a small hope that the world might not be over. I did not want to disturb the positive atmosphere of this trip. At least, it seemed to me that Beti and Karen were indifferent, or maybe we were all just playing together in front of each other, that we had nothing to worry about. Sometimes we have to act merriment and then it really settles in us, at least until the next day.

30

We finished the cruise in Masaka. A friend of Monica drove us to her house in her car. Monica and Sarrah, a friend from Dr Kendall, were sitting on the terrace. The look on their faces foreshadowed what they were about to say. Without unnecessary and superfluous words, we started the conversation. Almost unanimously, Brian and I asked:

"Where is Dr Kendall?"

"Dr Kendall is dead," Monica said in a low voice.

We were silent for a few moments, then Sarrah spoke up: "Thomas shot himself."

"How did that happen?" we wondered. Sarrah replied:

"Thomas immediately sought to continue the project you had started together when he learned of the death of your friends. He contacted his friend at the Ames Research Centre in Moffett Field. He even visited him in California. A friend introduced him to a scientist, Dr Mansfeld, who was a close colleague of Kamala and Joseph McCormack. Thomas was so impressed by him that he partially revealed himself to him. He didn't tell him everything, but enough for Mansfeld to figure out what was going on. Then he told Thomas that he had worked with the McCormacks, Al-Abadi and others. The tragic dinner, where all his colleagues were killed, was cancelled at the last minute due to his wife's sudden weakness. It saved their lives. Before Thomas returned home, he visited me in Seattle and told me the wonderful news he had brought back from America. A few days later, a mutual friend, a pilot who often flew from Victoria to Seattle, came to visit me. He told me that Thomas had shot himself in the head with a rifle. As he was able to find out, the same evening when he returned home, a number of armoured cars drove up in front of his house with police and armed people got out. He suspected something was very wrong, so he sat down in the armchair and pushed the shotgun in his mouth. I think Mansfeld betrayed him. They wanted to arrest him, and I can say with a fair degree of certainty that they intended to find out who all was involved in this conspiracy against the mafia by interrogating him, in order to prevent any unnecessary disruption and difficulties in the execution of their satanic plan. Maybe they are even following me and I have put you in danger by my visit here. But there is a chance that they do not know about me, and it is better that I inform you about this terrible accident, because you actually have no chance of completing your project. I am sure that you would be looking for Dr Kendall and then you would be caught, imprisoned, tortured and perhaps even killed. They want to thoroughly clean up anything that might threaten them."

"You did the right thing," I said in a voice that was not my own. It came from far away, from another world. "Mansfeld betrayed Kamala and Joseph. I am now convinced of that. It's over, I suspected it."

"You're right, Mansfeld is theirs," said Brian. "What David and I suspected is now confirmed. The end of hope for the world."

Monica said:

"Dr Kendall was a great man. By taking his own life, he saved our lives. The future is uncertain, but we still have hope, however tiny, but it is still alive."

"David and I are planning to move to Australia together. I have a large property in the west of the country where we can live self-sustainably far from the chaos that will reign on Earth. I invite you to join us," said Brian.

First Monica answered, then Sarrah:

"I'm staying here, with my people. I'm not going anywhere. This is my home. I don't want to leave them now, when they need me most."

"I'm going back to Seattle too. I will end my life where I started it. My son and daughter and their families need me. Thank you for your generous invitation, but I cannot extinguish their hope for the future."

"I understand," said Brian. I said to Monica:

"When I return to Europe from Uganda, I will transfer you some money for you and your work."

"Thank you, we'll really need it."

We said goodbye to Monica and Sarrah. Monica's friend took us to Kampala the same day. We stayed there for a few more days to discuss how we were going to tackle the Halls Creek project. Brian and Karen returned to Melbourne, and we went to Geneva first. I made all the necessary arrangements at the bank to transfer the money to Australia, and I sent some money to Monica, as I promised. Spring was coming to Geneva. I remembered last spring in this city, when my life was turned upside down. Maybe it would have been better if I hadn't known. But now I know and I can't change it. We returned home and started preparing to leave for Australia. I sold all the possessions I had and the ones I inherited from my mother. There was enough money, but why would I need it?

31

At the beginning of July, we travelled to Melbourne. Ana and Rudi travelled with us and managed to sell everything.

On the way to Australia, we stopped for a few days in Copenhagen, where I met Marghrete. I wanted to talk to her before we were lost in the Australian wilderness. Beti was with her parents sightseeing in the capital of Denmark, northern Paris, as some call it, and I met my friend at her home. I've always loved Marghrete, even though we never got into the bed together. She was a bit older than me. In fact, she was a kind of role model for me. A woman who knew no obstacles, or rather, overcame them as a joke. She had found a solution for every problem. I doubted that she had the solution to our problem, but I had to tell her what was happening in the world. I took my time and told her everything. She never doubted my words for a moment.

"Uh David, this is a supernova," said Marghrete, when I had finished telling her about the nano-catastrophe. "In fact, we can only watch the planet collapse until it swallows us too."

"I'm going to Australia with Beti and her parents to stay with my friend Brian. You can join us."

"No, I will not withdraw from this world. I'm going to be a robot," she replied, ironically and humorously. "Maybe if I were healthy, I would go down there with you. Unfortunately, my fate has other plans for me. Cervical cancer has grown inside me. I'm waiting for treatment, maybe surgery. I don't know what will happen to me. In fact, it would suit me to get out of here and die in the wild, but I would only be a burden to you."

"What do you say, cancer is eating you up. My mother also fell ill and…" I interrupted a sentence.

"Tell me until the end, she died. I'm going to die too, and don't think you can escape death by fleeing to Australia. We will all die; some from disease, others as robots and you who are out there somewhere will be eaten by the beasts," she joked. "Where did your mother get this parasite?"

"The pancreas."

"The worst chance of survival. I am not afraid of the disease, but I have read everything there is to read about it. I want to know what I am up against. That's why I know that pancreatic cancer is the deadliest. Maybe it's better to be killed faster and not suffer for months or years with the disease. What did we talk about?"

"You told me why you're not coming to Australia with me."

"Yes, that's my diagnosis. Have you ever thought that maybe we could get this project of the devil's emissaries into the media, among the people?"

"I am, but anyone who did would be signing his own death warrant. They would have liquidated him immediately, just like they did Dr Kendall."

"I can do it in such a way that no one will know where it came from."

"If you have the option not to endanger yourself, then I don't see any problem. But I am sure there will be no effect because the masters will make sure that the information is diluted the moment it appears in the world. Either they will simply block them, or they will release a hundred other pieces of information into the media, and then people won't know what is real and what is not, and the apocalypse that is hanging over us will become one of the conspiracy theories."

"It costs me nothing to try. I'll have fun with it. But maybe the information will fall on fertile ground somewhere and grow into something bigger. I know that these creatures hold all the threads of this world in their hands, but I will do it for you and for me."

"OK. Do what you can do without putting yourself at risk. They will not kill you immediately. You will be kidnapped and tortured until you betray me. This could be done with hypnosis or medieval methods. Their goals sanctify all their means."

"I have the ability to distribute information to all major media outlets around the world without the mafia finding out where it comes from."

"Are you sure you can do something like this in a digitalised world of the twenty-first century without being tracked?"

"I'm sure, trust me."

"I trust you."

"When you're in Australia, watch the world media and you'll be surprised. There will probably be an immediate attack from their side, but the diversion will happen, and at least for a few hours, the devils will be out of their minds."

"When are you going to do it?"

"In five days' time, go online and read everything you can read. You will see my work. That's better than the chemotherapy I'm probably going to have. If I didn't want to put you and your friends at risk, I would be happy to sign the article I'm going to send into orbit. Don't be afraid."

I took her hand and said: "I trust you, Marghrete." She smiled and said:

"So, now we've done it. When are you heading to Melbourne?"

"Tomorrow evening."

"Good, now tell your wife and her parents that they won't see you today. I will kidnap you. We'll drink for our farewell."

I did not want to contradict her. It was a pleasure to spend an evening with Marghrete. She was a pleasant interlocutor for the various philosophical questions that regularly came up between us in our alcohol-induced state.

First we had a vegetarian dinner, Marghrete was a vegetarian and I let her guide me through the labyrinth of vegetarianism. The Italian wine warmed us up. After dinner, we emptied a few more bottles of ruby wine, then moved to the bar, where drinks were served until the morning.

"When did you get married?" she asked me.

"I'm not married, we are partners, lovers, two living together."

"Then I misunderstood you. I was in a long relationship with a man I thought we would be together with until the end. When he found out that I had cancer, he told me that he didn't want to hurt me, but that he hadn't felt anything for me for a long time. A real man, that's for sure."

"He will fry in hell."

"He's already frying. Just a few days after we broke up, he had a car accident. He died with a female passenger who had his penis in her mouth."

I laughed at someone else's misfortune. Marghrete laughed too.

"I didn't want him to, but karma can throw surprises at you. When we meet up there he'll probably squeal and jump around me, but unfortunately I'll have to turn him down because I'm not a lesbian."

We both started to guffaw and I accidentally knocked over a glass, which fell off the counter and shattered. Marghrete grabbed her glass and dropped it on the floor. We laughed even more and kept drinking. After a while, she took my hand and said:

"We never fell together. Why not?"

"I don't know, you didn't like me."

"I liked you and I still do, but I guess we never felt the need to have sex." I thought she was trying to seduce me, but she wasn't.

"I would fuck you today, but I can't anymore. There is no more sex for me in this world. The pain in the lower region is constant. Despite the pills and the wine, the animal is gnawing in my belly. Don't worry about me. We'll have sex in the next life."

I did not know what to say to her. Marghrete broke the silence.

"Tell me, what are you going to do down there with the Aborigines?"

"We will live like the first immigrants. We will more or less depend on ourselves and our work. No electronics, no internet, no cars…We have a small plane that can take us to a nearby town. We'll farm, raise animals, have sex and drink," I said in a wavering voice, and raising my glass.

"Here's to us and our sex in the life to come."

"To sex," said Marghrete, and drunk up her glass of wine.

"I could be a farmer too, milking cows, shearing sheep, making cheese and all the things you can do on a farm, but the man upstairs has other plans for me. I do not complain about karma and I have no regrets. That's fucking life, and I should have thought about milking before," Marghrete said, laughing. Soon her laughter turned into a giggle. She hugged me and said, "I still want to live, but I have no control over that. Why is life so fucked up and full of injustice, but at the same time worth living? Maybe I'll find out when I'm released like smoke into the air from the chimney of the crematorium. I'll come and tell you. Right?"

"Come, I'd be glad if you'd visit me," I replied in a shaky voice. My lacrimal glands started producing huge amounts of tears. We kissed. We shared a long kiss. A kiss of goodbye to each other, goodbye to the world, goodbye to life. The kiss we shared was full of pain, bitterness and forgiveness at the same time. Then we drank some more. I don't remember when we got home. We slept until noon. The time had come for that final act, the time to say goodbye. I was like a tree. My head was a mess of the previous evening's events, emotions and painful goodbyes. I couldn't move for a while, then I hugged her.

"Goodbye Marghrete."

"Goodbye David, follow the media."

"I will."

"I'll see you later."

"Definitely."

Part 2

1

On the plane to Melbourne via Dubai, I had Marghrete on my mind. I told Beti everything. I just kept the sex talk quiet. She understood me and let me be myself on the flight. Whenever I am confronted with existential questions, I begin to question the meaning of life. Again and again. Then I take time to think, and I always come to a conclusion that is similar to what Socrates supposed to say: "Live as if there were an afterlife and earn it by living exemplarily. If it doesn't exist, you have nothing to lose." Live, don't give up. Falling down and getting up, again and again. Terry Jacks' song echoed in my head:

Goodbye Marghrete, it's hard to die when all the birds are singing in the sky now that the spring is in the air.
With the flowers everywhere, I wish that we could be there.

After arriving in Melbourne, we all gathered at Brian's house to discuss how we would go about this unique project of retreating into the wild to protect ourselves from enslavement or an early death. Anna and Rudi immediately became friends with Doctors Susan and Michael, Brian's parents. They had agreed to join us on this odyssey. Together, they set off on a cruise around Australia; Brian, Karen, Beti and I set about setting up our accommodation and stockpiling the necessities of life on the property. Michael provided us with a helicopter with a pilot to facilitate the transport of goods from Halls Creek to the property we called the ranch.

We stayed in Melbourne for about a month. Brian had arranged all the necessary paperwork, including our visas, which should no longer be needed once we're tucked away in our cocoons in Halls Creek. Every day, we followed the world's media on the internet in small internet cafés. We caught an interesting text called Armageddon, sent to the world by Marghrete. In a short text, she described everything that was in the plans of the global elite. Finally, she warned people to be cautious and to resist the genocide that is about to take place as best they can. The next day, Armageddon was nowhere to be seen online. We saw a pamphlet on all media portals that completely undermined Margrethe's efforts and labelled it as a harmful virus that had gone viral on the web. We knew it was a futile attempt.

Once we were done in Melbourne, we flew to Halls Creek. There, we planned to take a close look at the existing buildings and the property and draw up plans for the layout of the buildings for our living quarters, for the animals and for the other necessary buildings needed by the future subsistence ranch. Then we started to procure and supply the materials needed to renovate the buildings. We had to be precise because of transport. The helicopter was a great help. It was used to transport all the necessary materials, tools and necessities.

We built an underground fuel tank on the ranch for our plane and for a small agricultural machine, which was flown in by helicopter with its accessories. We also built a solar power plant that provided enough electricity for our small village. Five buildings have been made habitable, some have been renovated and some have been extended. The main building material was timber, which we transported in large quantities from Halls Creek. Water was piped in from two nearby springs, which provided drinking water. We also built a large rainwater harvesting tank, and although there was little rain, it was precious water that we used for purposes that did not require drinking water, such as flushing toilets, laundry, watering and other uses in our daily work and life on the ranch. We hired extra labour to dig the underground storage. For foodstuffs that did not necessarily require very low temperatures for storage, we built a large enough underground storage facility.

By the end of the year, we had made all the necessary arrangements for subsistence living on the ranch and stockpiled enough supplies to last several years. However, we continued to purchase more durable foodstuffs. We also started raising livestock, small livestock, rabbits and poultry. We even had a fish pond. We made sure the animals were safe from outside predators.

We celebrated Christmas and New Year with Anna, Rudi, Susan and Michael, who had just returned from a trip. Vasili and his new friend, Alina, joined us.

Brian's parents had also set up a small clinic with all the necessary equipment for treatment, including instruments for minor surgery. They also made a stockpile of medicines, which they put together by their judgement. They were also good experts in Aboriginal medicine, so our health was well taken care of.

As we were on an estate with no internet, no mobile phone signal, we gave up all electronic devices. We practically lived cut off from the world. Brian and I flew to Halls Creek once or twice a week. Sometimes someone else joined us. Brian taught me how to fly the plane, so I was the pilot and he was the co-pilot. As long as we were able to fly, we had replenished our supplies with fresh food. We also got the news in Halls Creek.

There were no disagreements between us because we organised our lives in such a way that we could live without each other. Only on the larger works had we joined forces. There were also days when we didn't even meet. Beti and I lived in one house, Brian and Karen in another, Anna and Rudi in theirs, Susan and Michael and Vasili and Alina. We also built a new home for Klara and her partner and his daughter.

Life was peaceful; I could even say we lived in a primitive idyll. By the beginning of the following year, information was already starting to come in about the virus that had first affected people in Asia. People started dying. It started earlier than Brian and I had anticipated. The beginning of Armageddon.

2

We had been following the development of a pandemic caused by a virus that people used to call the black virus. The virus spread uncontrollably around the world. It also came to Australia. Halls Creek was a small town where people rarely came, especially during the movement restrictions that came with the pandemic, so there were no cases in the first wave. The restrictions that followed the outbreak were beyond our expectations from the start.

Individuals who resisted the long-prepared fascist dictatorship that reigned in the developed world and did not respect preventive measures to protect them from infection were punished. In the early months of the pandemic, people were lenient about the measures, but as the pandemic escalated, with more and more viruses that could not be stopped, people began to have questions that they did not have answers to. All sorts of conspiracy theories began to emerge, all of which were essentially true, but the world did not know it.

Klara decided to stay in Slovenia after the first wave because, after convincing her partner, she decided that the danger was over. But when she finally realised that this was not the case, and that we were right, it was too late for her. Because of the travel ban, and because Australia had closed in on itself, she couldn't come to Halls Creek. Ana and Rudi wanted to return to Slovenia after the first wave because of Klara's decision, but Beti and I convinced them to stay. Our community had been reduced by two members. Vasili and Alina returned to Russia after the first wave. Alina did not want to be a farmer, shut away from everything. She was young and naive. Vasili didn't care, as long as he was with her. When they were saying goodbye, he said he would be back. He did not return. We never found out what happened to him.

Monica and we have been corresponding electronically. It was possible to use the internet in Halls Creek. She had more and more work. In addition to the black virus, Uganda has also been plagued by other diseases. After five years, we never heard from her again.

We were increasingly isolated. We came to Halls Creek less and less often. The first wave was followed by a second, a third, a fourth and so on. Each successive one was worse than the last. New versions of viruses had been increasingly deadly. Vaccines have emerged that claimed to be successful against earlier versions of the black virus, but were not successful against newer versions. The world was spinning in a vicious circle. Initially, vaccinations were voluntary. Then the pressure mounted until vaccinations became compulsory. Those who insisted against vaccination were imprisoned in special camps, stripped of all their property and all their civil and human rights. Fascism ruled the world with a heavy hand. There were more and more dead people. Poor countries had been hardest hit. Their population had been severely decimated. They were deliberately left without vaccines, which would have prolonged their lives somewhat, and they were probably infected with more deadly viruses. The final solution was implemented according to the plans that Joseph and Kamala McCormack gave me in Geneva a few years ago. There were also demonstrations around the world, but they were violently repressed by the rulers at the cost of many deaths. The internet was our only link to the world, and after a few years it was shut down. From then on, the world was in darkness.

The virus also arrived in Halls Creek. Initially, only a small number of people were infected. We also respected the measures to prevent the spread of the virus when we came to Halls Creek. First, it was the mandatory surgical masks, then more and more sophisticated masks, and finally even special suits. The last time Brian and I were in Halls Creek, there were police officers in special suits patrolling the streets, shooting anyone who wasn't fully equipped for the new conditions. We quickly flew back to our ranch, one of the few oases, or even last refuge, for people who have not become robots or succumbed to disease at least until then.

3

On the ranch, we lived a life completely our own, independent of the outside world. The four households lived on their own, but we got together and worked together when necessary. Cereals, potatoes, maize and a few other crops were grown communally, while the rest was grown by each household. We had large gardens around our houses, which we looked after each in our own way. There were more and more livestock, and we were just there to supervise them and help with litters or illnesses. The animals were killed with a shotgun blast. At first, it was very unpleasant, but later we men got used to this thankless job. Cutting the meat was also a man's job, and the women were in charge of preserving and storing the meat and making the meat products, although we all did it together, but under their strict command. Karen was initially a vegetarian, but gradually returned to the meat. Sometimes we also went hunting, more for the enjoyment of life than out of necessity. The change in the menu was also welcome.

Occasionally, we spent evenings together on the veranda or in the garden of one of the houses. We made our own juices, even brewed and distilled our own beer and brandy. We also managed to produce wine. The fruit trees did very well, giving us compotes, jams and dried fruit as well as juices. We made sure that our food was as varied as possible. We were exercising with work, not so much that it would tire us too much. We worked as much as necessary to maintain the ranch and grow food.

We were healthy, but every now and then we got an injury at work, which was immediately treated by the doctors. Ana was bitten by a snake while gardening, but according to Brian, it was not so venomous that it seriously endangered her life. Rudi had a blood pressure problem, which the doctors successfully controlled with some medicine they got a prescription for from the Aborigines.

Brian and I had sterilisation in Melbourne to prevent pregnancy. Unfortunately, we could not afford children. Beti found this difficult to accept.

A child born in isolation would have no chance. If there were more couples on the ranch, then maybe we could plan our offspring. But there was no hope of survival. Karen was doubtful about getting pregnant at all. When she wanted to have a baby with her previous partner, doctors told her it would be very difficult to get pregnant. But Brian was sterilised anyway.

After a few years of living on the ranch, we were almost left without everything. It was afternoon and a storm was approaching. It started to thunder and lightning was shooting back and forth. One of them started a fire on a pile of straw, not far from the houses. The fire started to spread rapidly. Rudi took the initiative in extinguishing the fire and, at first; it seemed that we would manage to contain the fire. However, the wind scattered the mass of burning embers in a large circle around the centre of the fire. The vegetation was dry and burning like oil. When we had already surrendered, when the fire was close to the houses and the parked plane, it started pouring from the sky.

A cloud burst and a mass of large raindrops initially stopped the spread and, after a few hours of heavy rain, finally doused the fire. We saved ourselves, or we had been saved. After the fire, we thanked God for saving us from our misfortunes and asked Him to spare us new ones. In this sense, too, we had become primitive. I myself still had mixed feelings about believing in the supernatural, but over time I slowly began to believe in that which is above us and that it can spare scourges. But those up there did not hear us.

4

Of all members of our community in exile, Beti was the one who endured the space constraints the most. She was happy with the life we were living on the ranch. She took care of the house, the garden, and was always one of the first when we all got to work together. She told me several times that she had achieved the peace she had always wanted. Even the dry and hot climate couldn't stop her from enjoying it. The only thing she missed was her children. She wanted to have children with me. Unfortunately, we couldn't afford them. She understood, but here and there she was overcome by a sense of motherhood. We lived as husband and wife. One day, she said to me:

"David, let's get married."

"How should we get married?" I asked her.

"Right here. Brian, Karen, Susan, Michael, Dad and Mum, whoever can marry us, or all of them together."

We had a wedding in front of a gathering of the other six members of our big family and the Creator who watched over us. We were married. They also prepared a document that we signed together with our registrars, who signed our marriage certificate. The rings were given to us by Ana and Rudi. After the wedding, we had a wedding party, we even had music. We danced and laughed. I got married. This wedding was soon followed by another, Karen and Brian got married.

We needed to have fun at work. We celebrated everything there was to celebrate, from birthdays to anniversaries. We socialised, laughed and forgot about the prison we lived in. Ana and Rudi had the most problems. They were worried about Klara. Their mood fluctuated. Beti spent a lot of time with them. Rudi suffered a minor cardiac arrest, but no serious consequences. The older part of the community was well into their seventies. Susan and Michael were a little older than Anna and Rudi, but they coped better with the exile. Brian and I knew that the day would come when they would start leaving. Then we would also be without a doctor.

When Brian and I returned from our last trip to Halls Creek, we had brought the virus with us, or it had come to us by air. After a few years of living together, a serious illness came between us for the first time. Rudi was the first victim of the virus. At first, he was just tired, then he came down with a high fever. Susan and Michael helped him as much as they could under the circumstances. He suffered greatly in the last days of his life. He was breathing very heavily. Beti and Anna took care of him. They prayed that he would not suffer, and one morning the suffering was over. We had identified a site where we had built a small cemetery. That was the first time we realised the inevitable fate of every human being. When life ends, death comes. Brian and I made the coffin. We placed Rudi's body in it and lowered it into the grave. Beti summoned up enough strength to carry out a short funeral service. Then Brian and I filled in the grave and planted a wooden cross on the mound with the name and the year of birth and death. Beti was crying, Anna just stared blankly at the grave.

After the funeral, Brian and I left the cemetery.

"We all knew that without death there is no life, but until it came among us it was somewhere far away," I spoke, breaking the silence.

"The virus is among us, we're all going to leave, we just don't know the order," said Brian.

"I don't understand how it could have come among us. We watched the events in Halls Creek from a safe distance and when we saw the chaos in the streets and the killing, we immediately retreated. I suspect they know about our ranch and have decided to kill us."

"A few years ago, I would have disputed this hypothesis, but now I'm not convinced it's not true."

"What can we possibly do? Let's commit collective suicide or wait to fall one by one."

"I don't know. Maybe we should try to survive after all?"

"Do you think there's a chance?"

"I have spoken to my father and mother, who take the situation very seriously, but don't think it is necessary to give up. Our bodies react differently to viruses that attack them."

"I didn't mean to kill myself, but I still wonder what the point of persisting is. It's all hopeless. We have started burying the dead, and no one will bury the last one to die."

"I know it's all getting grotesque, but I convince myself that it's worth living to the end, breathing and living. There has to be some meaning to this life."

"Breathe and live. Sometimes I feel like getting on a plane and flying up into the sky to find a place where this virus does not exist. Maybe this place is waiting for us somewhere. Since we don't know, we have to believe. That is why we need to breathe and live. You are right. This is the meaning of life. To breathe and live and survive. If you live honestly and you are not at war with other people, with the universe, with yourself, you have nothing to fear when death comes. Now I know, but maybe tomorrow I'll be in doubt again."

"That's life in this world. Every day there are doubts, questions, and then you breathe again and go on living. The strongest triumph, and they are not afraid of life and its end. Death is feared by those whose life is a sham and a self-deception. They cling to life because they are afraid that then there is nothing more, that the darkness will overwhelm them. They are convinced of this, but in their subconscious they are filled with doubt, and their reaction is more egotism and anger at the whole world."

"Did you study theology?" I joked.

"I study it every day," he replied in the same tone, and then we parted.

That evening and long into the night, Beti and I talked. She was worried about who would be left alone. She was also shocked by the death, not only because Rudi was her father.

"David, I don't know how I would have survived if you had died before me, even though I would have wanted to suffer for us and not you. Those who remain will suffer. I wish you a long life, but when we have to say goodbye, let me suffer and I will come for you soon."

"My love, a long time may we both live. Today, you are under the impression of Rudi's death. We are not escaping death, but we are a long way from it," I told her firmly, but insincerely. Death was near and we were both aware of it. "Now we must look after each other and drive death from our ranch."

"If my father died from a virus that is supposed to be ravaging the world, then it is probably already among us and it is only a matter of time before one of us is the next to fall ill. It may well be that he was the weakest because of the heart attack and that is why it attacked him first. I hope I'm wrong."

"The cardiac arrest must have weakened his body."

"Is there anything we can do to resist this plague or should we just wait calmly for this microscopic little killer to attack us and surrender to it?"

"Let's leave that topic for another time. We must live and breathe. Every moment should be full of life, but when that last moment comes, we have to accept it. I also face similar questions every day. I am at the beginning again and again. Just when I think I've made a breakthrough, I'm back to the beginning. Then enlightenment comes again and I am sure I understand life and its meaning."

"I know, dear, we are going around in circles. Blessed are those who manage to get out of this crazy spin."

"Blessed are they. It's worth every day of our lives to try to get off this merry-go-round."

"We're going to get out. One way or another. I love you."

"I love you," then we fell asleep. We slept cuddled up all night. Sleep was not as sound as usual after a hard day, but she wanted me to hold her close and I was happy to oblige her.

5

The days after Rudi's death followed the same rhythm as all the days before. Just when we thought the virus was gone, that it had retreated, Ana fell ill. Gradually, she began to weaken. First, she retreated into seclusion, with only Beti coming to her. The disease progressed more slowly than with Rudi. For some time, the situation remained unchanged. There has been neither improvement nor deterioration. Beti looked after Ana, I did the jobs she usually did. Susan and Michael were helpless; they didn't know how to help Ana. Then her body crashed. She suffocated for three days, gasping for air, before she died. Her dying left Beti completely squeezed. I was afraid for her. My fears were justified. Beti fell ill a few days after we buried Ana. It's started. In a few weeks, we would all die.

Beti accepted her illness calmly. She knew what was in store for her. She just wanted me to be there and talk to her.

"You know David," she started the conversation, "it was nice to be with you. I have been waiting for you since I was fifteen. I knew the day would come when our love would blossom. I waited twenty years, but never once doubted that we would not be together one day. In life, some things happen that you know will happen when they are ripe, and that reassures you. When you are calm, you don't make mistakes, you live. I knew; that's why I lived. I know you've had a lot of women, and I wasn't totally innocent either. But that didn't make me doubt for a moment, because I knew that our souls were more connected than people could imagine. I am aware that we will soon be separated. But this separation will only be temporary. Even if you live another hundred years on Earth, it's only a fragment, just a yocto against a yotta, ten to minus twenty-four against ten to twenty-four. We have an eternity ahead of us and I am sure of it."

I thought she was feverish and grabbed her forehead. She touched my hand and said:

"I'm not hallucinating, if that's what you're thinking. I am speaking in full consciousness and what I have to say to you is not just empty words to encourage you to live on when I am gone, but I am speaking to you from my deepest insights and convictions. Don't be afraid. Everything will be fine. One path ends and another begins."

"How can you know what happens to us after we die?" I interrupted.

"I just know. The human spirit is not made of atoms and molecules. Matter changes, spirit remains. My body is a collection of cells that will disintegrate when I die. My spirit gave them life, but when it leaves the body, the cells perish. How can something as magnificent as the spirit, the human soul, be dissolved. When God said that He created man in His own image, He was not referring to the body, but to that which dominates the body. It is the soul, with its helper, mind, that gives life to the body. What separates us from animals is the soul. They too have a mind of their own, which varies from species to species. Animals also have a strong instinct, which we humans neglect because we rely too much on our minds. It is an inner sense, an inner eye to receive signals from the environment. Our bodies are like animal bodies, they work on the same principle. We reproduce in a similar way. But the upgrade that lifts us up and makes us one with the Creator is the soul. And it is eternal. That is why I have no doubt that death is not the end, but a new beginning."

"If we are eternal as you say, then why are we born into this world of suffering and uncertainty?"

"First of all, I want to tell you that when I talk about the spirit and the soul, it is the same for me. Some people separate the two, but in essence they are one. The spirit or soul is an autonomous spiritual being, but one that derives from the Creator and His love. Like all things in the material world, in the spiritual world there is a beginning and an end."

I interrupted her again:

"How does the soul have a beginning and an end, if you are talking about eternity?"

"Slow down, David. Human words can hardly describe the truth that is upon us. Our minds and our understanding are very limited, so it is difficult to grasp what eternity means. We measure everything in this world, we weigh everything. This is not the case in eternity. I can explain it to you in a language that is understandable to a being at this stage where we are human. The eternal spirit, the eternal intelligence, the eternal love manifests itself in different ways. There are countless variations through which the Creator manifests. Countless universes, countless galaxies, countless stars. Universes are not only material, they are also spiritual. The spiritual world is not seen with the eyes in the head, but with the inner eye.

There is supposed to be no life on Mars. But are we sure? Maybe our perception is so limited that we cannot perceive life there with our senses. Maybe there are beings among us on Earth that we simply do not see or hear. But they can see and hear us well. Anything is possible. The most incredible thought that comes to you is very vivid and real, but you can't catch it, you can't see it, so it seems like a delusion, like a fantasy. The saying that stuck in my mind when I was searching and researching, reading different texts, different thoughts, different experiences, is very true: 'Be careful what you think about, because thoughts can be creative'. So everything is real, both matter, antimatter, and thought, imagination. Everything exists. Maybe I got a little carried away, but I just wanted to say that it's all very complicated and simple at the same time. I will try to answer your question. So the Creator manifests Himself in different ways. The creation of the Universe, the galaxy, the sun and ultimately, the Earth, for example. Then comes the first life, which arises from acids and so on, all the way to the first plants and simple animal species. Species are evolving and becoming more and more prone to growth. In this diversity of living beings and innumerable variations, a being evolves that is similar to the human being of today, and this being is already ready to receive the soul. A human being is created. Man then evolves further and becomes more and more creative, relying more and more on his mind, which is the result of material evolution. But he forgets his spirit, which has taken up residence in his body. The soul that takes up residence in the body is the seed of the Creator, a part of Him. The human mind is a greatness to which we humans succumb and forget the spirit that is above it. Let's say smart people, scientists, invented a terrible weapon that required maximum mental capacity from them. But they have created a means to kill other creatures, to destroy lives, which is contrary to eternal love, to creation and to the Creator Himself. So their mind has taken precedence over their spirit. They do not care about destroying lives, but only about achieving selfish goals. But this is contrary to eternal unity. That is why our history is so bloody and why we learn so little from it. But that doesn't mean that all people are like that. Unfortunately, in most cases, these are the people who rule our world. That is why they came up with this madness we are witnessing now, to rule the world and get rid of superfluous and unnecessary people. The negative beings present in our world, some call them the devil, have a powerful influence on people who, although free thinkers, are tempted by wealth, fame and power at the cost of the suffering of others. They succumb to an evil spirit, a deceitful serpent. And that is how they get caught in the loop. They have to go through this stage again in the evolution of the spirit that we are in in this world, which is the lowest of the stages in the growth of the spirit. People are free to choose whether to grow in spirit, stagnate or even decline. Regression means that the soul goes to a lower world than the one in which it lived, even though it had the possibility of advancement or at least the possibility of rebirth or purification, as Christianity says. Some religions speak of reincarnation, of being born again, some of purgatory, which is basically repeating life as many times as necessary until the soul progresses to a higher level. This can mean many births, many lifetimes, until the individual soul is ripe for advancement. Rebirth does not necessarily mean birth in this world as we know it, but it can be birth in the same world as ours, where souls are at the same level. But if a soul progresses to a higher level, it means that it is going to a higher world. Religions talk about heaven, about nirvana, which is not accurate. The soul goes to a higher stage and from there again progresses gradually through innumerable stages until it returns to oneness, to the Creator. That is why I talk about the beginning and the end, although there is no beginning, but that is the easiest way to describe this journey in words that are understandable at this stage. There is no beginning and no end, but only variations, deviations, or different manifestations of creation, which represent our path from the moment we leave the Creator and return to Him. But we are always connected to Him, like a child in his mother's womb. If we walk away from Him and cut the umbilical cord with Him, then we are lost and doomed. The worst part is that those who choose this path for themselves then realise it when it is too late and they are forged alive in eternal ice, if I can borrow a metaphor."

"Why don't we remember our past lives so that we don't make the same mistakes in our new life as we did in our previous ones?"

Beti smiled. I was amazed by her narrative and her conviction in the words she spoke.

"If we could remember our past lives, then it would be easy. We would correct our mistakes and we would move on, even though we have not grasped the essence of life, the essence of spiritual life and spiritual growth. It's like copying your classmate's results in a test at school and getting a high mark for it, even though you have no idea about the topic in the test. Every spiritual being, and we humans are first and foremost spiritual beings, needs only to know the way and the truth. That is why the Creator does not help us directly. We have to make our own choices, our free will takes us forward, and turns us around in circles or dooms us. Even when we suffer, the Creator does not intervene in our lives. This is also the answer when some people ask why God does not help us, if He really exists. Of course, He exists, but because we are free beings with free will, it is up to us to decide whether we return to Him or fall away from Him forever. If you help yourself, God will help you, or in other words, first you have to know your essence, with the help of religions, teachers, holy books, contemplation, meditation, even science and art, and then the path will always be easier. Along the way, you have to observe the signs that the Creator sends us, encouraging us to keep going. Or it warns us that we have strayed from the path. But if we are not paying attention, if we are too self-absorbed and too much of a god unto ourselves, then our eyes and our ears are blind and deaf to these signs. And we will be born so many times until we get on the right path.

When we die physically, our soul enters the world where we meet our deceased relatives, friends and acquaintances. That's why some people talk about the light at the end of the tunnel, because the soul gets into a beautiful world, into heaven if you like. But it is only a waiting room from where we go on to a higher dimension, back to birth or to eternal imprisonment. When we go into rebirth, the memory of our previous lives is erased, frozen and we start again. When we die and come to this in-between world, we remember all our lives. That's why we always start again until we have matured and passed all the exams for promotion. If we look deep into ourselves and into our souls, we can peer into this world at the end of the tunnel and become aware of the mistakes we are making and have made in previous lives. But we can spoil everything."

I didn't want to ask her anymore, even though I had a thousand questions, she was too tired. She soon fell asleep.

We continued to talk over the next few days, but the conversations were always shorter. Her strength was failing, her voice was getting quieter. Beti was leaving. She left a few days later. For me, her death was the end of everything, the end of the world. All those words of hers about eternity and eternal love had evaporated. She was no longer among the living, and that was a fact for me, a cruel fact. I loved her, I loved her all my life, but I came to her late, too late. We should have been together for many years, we should have enjoyed life. I hoped to die soon myself and go after her. Maybe I will meet her again, or maybe she was just saying that to prepare me for my death.

There were terrible days for me. I had so many things to reproach myself for, but I couldn't change anything anymore. When we buried her, I stayed all night at her grave and talked to her. I told her everything. I told her that I had always loved her too, but I didn't dare to admit it because I wanted to live in an illusion, because I wanted to go crazy. Because I preferred sex, pleasure, wandering around the world, to true love. I was afraid of real life, which was life beside her and with her. I gave in to the illusion that the only thing that counts in this life is enjoyment. But it all went past me. I don't even remember what I did with my life anymore, but I remember the time I spent with her. I begged her for forgiveness. I heard her voice saying to me:

"I have nothing to forgive you. We came together and that's the most important thing."

I mourned her; I will mourn her for the rest of my life.

6

Nothing was the same anymore. A plague came to our small community and started killing us. The next two on its list were Susan and Michael. They said goodbye in silence. They cared for each other until the end. First he left, and then, a few days later she left. There were only three of us left. Me, Karen and Brian.

This is what it was. Who would be the next? Who would be the last? Brian and I made three more coffins, although the last one would probably stay where he died. We were condemned to death, the day of execution was unknown, but it was steadily approaching. Brian was still more cheerful than me, maybe because he had Karen. I was left alone. On the evening of the day of Susan's funeral, we sat outside his house, drinking homemade concoctions.

"David, I think I'm next," he started the conversation. "What makes you say that?"

"I feel I have come to the end. Karen will outlive me, but you obviously can live with this virus."

"Why do you think I'm immune to the virus?"

"You were together with Beti until her death. You cared for her and took care of her. Apparently, your body is producing antibodies that are successfully defending you against attacks by the black virus for the time being."

"For the time being, I don't know why I don't get sick. My antibodies may indeed be successful, but how much longer they will be able to fight off viral attacks is unknown. Maybe the one up there, who is supposed to take care of us, is deliberately torturing me until I come to reconciliation with myself, with the world and with him. I would like to live, but that's not for me to decide. I can decide, if I'm the last one, to leave on my own when I decide to do so."

"Would you kill yourself?"

"No, but it is also an option in a moment of diminished presence of mind, weakness and fatigue."

"Unfortunately, I agree with you. I don't know how I would react if I were sentenced to life in solitary confinement. In prison, you would see prison guards, but here you are all alone. You can surrender to the masters and their toadies, and be roboticised or euthanized. I don't know what's worse. I think it's the least bad thing, though, to live here alone until your hour comes."

"You are right. If someone had told me before this shit what we were in for, I would probably have referred him for a detailed psychiatric examination. What happened to us was unimaginable, unfathomable, and unconscionable."

"It's really crazy. What's even crazier is that we retreated into isolation and managed to escape a death sentence for a few years. If we hadn't hidden, we would be dead by now, or we would have become robots."

"I'm R2D2 and you're C3PO," I joked.

"I don't know what I would be; I know I wouldn't be me. And that's the point of this escape; I will stay until the end. We are indeed restricted in our movements, but we still live with a certain degree of freedom. I cannot imagine being imprisoned in a concentration camp because I refused to be vaccinated, where I would sooner or later be killed or forcibly vaccinated."

"I agree with you, that's what escape is all about. To live freely to the end."

"I thought about what the world would be like today if we had succeeded with that vaccine back then."

"We could buy a couple of years, maybe ten or twenty. But sooner or later, the tyrannosaurs would find a way to destroy us. A global conspiracy is hard to fight. But it's also true that there is a chance of survival as long as you are alive and well. Unfortunately, it didn't happen. Joseph was very cautious, but he came across a tyrannosaur servant. They were great people. Whether fate, which is in the hands of the devil, intervened, or whether it was just a coincidence. We will never know."

"We had assembled a team of excellent people who could resist this plague. Dr Kendall was an extraordinary man who did more than he promised. What a cruel fate befell him when he met the McCormacks' executioner."

"He judged himself. He did not want others to decide his fate. In a similar situation, I would probably do the same. Just like us, except that we found a way out. I never asked you what the name of the ranch where we live is."

"It didn't have a name; I called it 'paradise'. We can give it a name now."

"I have a name: Atlantis."

"Atlantis?"

"Yes, a fitting name for our ranch, for with us will disappear the civilization that created this world."

"OK. Atlantis."

"But I always wonder if there is a person in the world who is like us, who has outcast ourselves."

"Maybe one of those who knew about the conspiracy, like us, has gone into seclusion. But I think the masters have taken good care to protect this great secret. After Joseph and Kamala and their friends paid expensively for their involvement, they were even more cautious. I even think they would have gotten to us eventually if we hadn't pulled out in time."

"We were very lucky. We must also thank Joseph and Kamala, who made sure we were more or less safe at all times. We didn't use telephones, we changed locations, and there was no correspondence between us."

"Can you imagine what the world is like out there right now? How many people are left in the world, how many are already roboticized, how many are waiting to die in a camp, how many are dead."

"Probably the poorer areas, the Middle East, Africa, South America, India and South-East Asia, were cleaned up first. It was where most of the poorer people lived, and to the tyrannosaurs they were just insects, weeds to be uprooted. Then they went ahead and did the selection. There are no free people anymore, only imprisoned people waiting to be executed, or they have become obedient androids. Maybe they even know about us, which is why they sent us the virus. It could have been dropped by a drone, or it could have been dispersed in some other way, even though we are harmless to them."

"I also doubt that we brought the virus from Halls Creek. Maybe they are watching us now, or maybe even listening. Technology has probably advanced to the point where they are looking at every single ant, every single mosquito on the globe."

"I wouldn't be too surprised if it's all true, what you say. Satellites scan every square centimetre of the Earth's surface, computers detect and record any anomalies, and report them to their masters. I'm sure they know about us. But we are harmless to them. But they sent us a shipment of viruses just in case."

"If I got on a plane and flew up into the sky, I would definitely be shot down. A satellite would have shot me in an instant with a laser beam."

"Who are the unfortunate elect who have been chosen to serve? I might even know someone from them. And they are happy now? They work, they earn and they have a good time. They are happy to be alive, unaware that they have become robots, their minds controlled and processed by tyrannosaurs according to their own plans and needs. They don't realise that they are not even human anymore."

"I think we should write about what has happened to this planet, about the world that once was."

"Who should we write for, aliens?"

"I don't know. I don't think it would be superfluous."

"You start, I'll continue when you're dead," I wanted to be witty.

"I take you at your word," said Brian, smiling.

A few days later, he fell ill too. He did not torture himself for long. Karen and I buried him in our cemetery. "Now it's really over," I thought.

"He was sick," said Karen. "He didn't want to tell you. Something was happening to his lungs. He coughed a lot, and the nights were particularly agonising for him. He hid his illness for three months. That's why the virus seemingly killed him so quickly."

"I wonder how I didn't notice or suspect that something was happening to him. He just told me that he was next. So it was not a matter of sense, but of awareness. Poor Brian. He was my best friend."

Karen and I both had tears running down our cheeks. We stared at the grave for a long time, letting the tears fall.

A few days later I moved in with Karen. It was just the two of us, so we agreed to live together. We also slept together. We were sure that neither Brian nor Beti would object. We were the last. The end of the world was approaching.

7

We lived together for three months. We gave in to our passions and until she fell ill, we had sex every day, several times a day. It was our drug, morphine, which eased the pain.

Karen had always seemed to me to be a strong woman who was not moved by anything. In fact, she was a very soft soul who was not spared life until she met Brian. She did not know her father. He was an American soldier in Okinawa who came to the Philippines for a holiday and met her mother there.

They fell in love immediately. He had to return to his military base on a Japanese island, but he was returning to the Philippines. One day, when her mother told him she was pregnant, he decided to leave the army and move in with her. He went to Okinawa one last time. He was not back. Mum thought he had left her. She gave birth to Karen. They lived in poverty. When Karen was five, her mother married a Filipino man and thought she could start a family with him and Karen would have a father. He was a corrupt man who drank and gambled all day long. He beat her mother, he beat Karen. Her mother decided to run away with her to Australia. Friends and relatives helped them. An US Army officer was on board the flight to Australia. He sat next to her mother and they soon got into a conversation. She learned that he lived and worked in Okinawa, so she immediately asked him about Air Lieutenant Bradley Strong, Karen's father. He remembered him and said that Lieutenant Strong had died in a plane crash. Her mother was relieved to hear this. He had not left her.

In Australia, they started again. Her mother worked, Karen went to school and took care of the household herself. The day she graduated from university, her mother died. Cardiac arrest stopped her joy. Karen then moved to Melbourne, where she met Brian, a few years later. She was a journalist, like us.

When Karen told me her story, I thought about all the things we carry with us through life. What stories, what novels every life writes. It's hard to describe our relationship. I was not in love with her, but I loved her very much. She was the last person I spoke to, the last woman I touched, and the last woman I made love to. That time we were together we forgot about the cruel and inevitable future. After three months of living together, when we were both widowed, after three months of the paradise we had created for ourselves, Karen fell ill. I took care of her day and night. I hoped and prayed for a miraculous cure. She didn't want to leave either. She didn't want to leave me. Her suffering lasted much longer than that of others. I slept next to her, kissing and caressing her. I wanted the viruses that reigned in her body to get inside me and kill me.

I slept very little with her. But that day, that morning, I slept soundly. When I woke up, I looked at her and stroked her. Her skin was cold. A scream burst out of me, cutting through the silence in which I was left alone. It was a cry of pain, a cry of despair, a cry of realisation, a cry of the last man. I was left alone. I was alone in the middle of the Australian wilderness. And worst of all, I was perfectly healthy. The virus didn't want me.

I brushed Karen's hair and put a red flower in her thick black hair. Although she was severely crippled by illness, she was beautiful. She was alive, just asleep. I sat next to her and held her hand. I couldn't let it go; I couldn't admit to myself that I was alone. I don't know how long I sat by her. Late in the afternoon, I went to the cemetery and dug a grave for her and myself. In the evening, I brought her body to the cemetery and put it in the coffin I had lowered into the shallow grave. Before I put the lid on the coffin, I showered her with flowers and kissed her again. I wanted to say something, but the words wouldn't come out. I lost my last woman, my second wife, with whom I lived together for only a short time. But what hurt and hurt the most was that I lost the last person with whom I breathed the same air, the person I touched, the person I talked to, and the person I made love to.

I filled in the grave, planted a cross and also strewed the fresh mound with colourful flowers. I wrote on the cross, Karen – the last woman and penultimate free man in the world. The next day I placed a coffin in the second grave I had dug, which I dedicated to myself, and at the head of it, I planted a cross on which was written: 'The last free man in the world, born in the year one thousand nine hundred and eighty-two, died in the year two thousand and two ix'. Whether my bones were in a grave or somewhere else didn't matter. Once I had done that, I got drunk and fell asleep.

8

For a few days after Karen died, I walked up and down the estate, because just walking was somewhat calming. I was getting further and further away from the ranch. I used to be out in the wild all day. Walking and nature, the many animals I met, brought me back to a state that allowed me to think. First, I checked my food supplies. It was enough, because death quickly mowed down the population of our settlement. I realised that only work and an active life would save me from the frenzy of loneliness. I euthanized some animals and made meat products from their flesh, which would last for a few months.

Then I decided to start writing. I have written my story. I wrote every day for over a month and finally got to where I am now. Apart from writing, my days were filled with daily walking and working on the ranch. I undertook various repairs and other small jobs that were not about the need for a job, but about keeping me busy. I took care of the animals and tended my garden.

I lived in Brian's house, which I made my own. There were two pictures on the wall above the bed, one of Beti, the other of the four of us, Brian, Karen, Beti and me. I also used the other houses, and set up my storage, laundry and workshop in them. I stored what I thought I needed, and the rest, especially the excess clothes, I burnt up. I also started sewing and patched and repaired what needed to be patched and repaired. I was lucky with the footwear, because all the men had about the same size feet. There was enough work, but I didn't overdo it, because I wasn't in a hurry to get anywhere. I stopped shaving, and I let my hair grow freely.

When everything was more or less done, I went to the hangar and tried to start the plane's engine. It didn't work. I dressed up as an aircraft mechanic and disassembled the engine, taking a detailed inventory of all the parts and the disassembly process. I cleaned and put everything back together. Then I checked the rest of the aircraft and found the fault. The rubber hose that feeds the fuel into the engine has decayed. I replaced it and tried the ignition. I did it. Then, every day, I took an aerial tour of the estate. I was not worried about the risk of being shot down...

Every evening before dark, I visited our cemetery and took care of the graves. I always did a small service for the dead there, which was a mixture of Christian prayers, with Islamic, Jewish and Buddhist elements. I thanked God for my friends and for everything He had offered me in my life. I kept saying in prayer that I was ready to die. But He did not hear me. My body was immune to viruses. I was healthy. I also started meditating. As soon as I got up in the morning, I sat down on the floor in front of the house and let the waves coming from space wash over me. I managed to find some much needed peace within myself, not completely, but here and there I soothed and calmed down. I energised myself by working, writing, walking and meditating. I was breathing at the top of my lungs. Nevertheless, sometimes a day would creep into my life and make me cry and give up. But I did not give up. I was alive.

There were many animals roaming around the ranch, and the dingoes were very active. Sometimes I had to shoot in the air with a shotgun and chase them away. Brian and I made a fence to protect the ranch and our animals from intruders. The fence was made of very thick wire mesh, so that only ants could sneak onto the ranch, although snakes sometimes came to visit, probably through an underground tunnel. There were many species of birds on the estate and all around Halls Creek, a paradise for ornithologists. I also became a connoisseur of the birds that nested on the ranch, or just came to visit. With the help of books I found in Brian's library, I was able to name them correctly. This introduced me to different species of parrots. I was particularly fascinated by the nymphs, then the owls, owl relatives with frog mouths, little honeyeaters, woodswallows, bee-eaters, miners. The nearby lake was also visited by kingfishers, herons, waders, numerous ducks and many other birds that I don't want to bother you with here.

As I fired my rifle to scare away the uninvited guests, thousands of birds flew into the sky and I scared them away. The shrieking voices of the frightened birds also disturbed the animals we had at the ranch. I rarely used a rifle, but for my safety and well-being, I always had it with me when I walked around the ranch, or left it when I went wandering. A big problem was the once domesticated animals that roamed freely in Halls Creek after the extinction of humans. Once, I came across a pack of feral dogs. I chased them away with several consecutive shots. There were also a lot of cats. Here and there I also came across cattle, sheep, goats and even poultry. All these animals would be completely wild in a few generations.

I have written down more or less everything that has happened so far. From now on, I will take notes in the form of a diary until the day I can no longer pick up a pencil. If you ask me about death. I have come to terms with that fact. But as long as I breathe, I will breathe with full lungs. I no longer think about suicide. I am aware that I can be kidnapped by illness or an accident. Then I will find it hard to look after myself. But I will fight as long as I can.

The Creator and I have become friends. I believe in the afterlife and in reuniting with my mother, with Beti, with Karen, with Brian, with Anna, with Rudi, with Susan, with Michael, with Monica, with Kamala, with Joseph, with Dr Kendall, with Marghrete and others. Maybe I'll meet Vasili there too. Whether I deserved promotion to the higher realms or another birth, I don't know.

But I am confident that I have paid for my sins and will not have to be forged in eternal ice. In addition to the services in the cemetery, I have also arranged shorter services before every work and before every meal. I do not ask anything of the Creator, I just thank Him. I am in contact with Him all the time. He keeps me company and helps me not to go mad.

Part 3

The Day I Started Writing My Diary

I woke up at sunrise, just like every day. After a morning meditation and a plane ride, I went for a walk around the ranch. I also walked a little outside the fence. Everything was fine. After lunch and an hour's rest, I set about repairing the shelves in the underground storage room and taking control of the stock. I've had enough sugar and salt for more than twenty years. Canned fruit and vegetables were also plentiful. Salt and sugar were stored in metal containers. Evening prayer in the cemetery. After dinner, I sat outside the house for a long time, listening to the night voices. In the distance to the west, lightning could be seen. The rain was coming.

Day 2

Lightning struck somewhere on the ranch and woke me up. It started to rain heavily. As it was still night, I was lying in bed. I managed to fall asleep. When I woke up, the daylight was very dim because it was still raining. I did meditation in the house. Then I started reading. Late in the afternoon, the rain stopped. I went to the cemetery and the ground was soaked. The reservoir was full of water, which I will need for the bathroom and for watering the garden. It was a clear evening and I couldn't sleep for a long time. Loneliness was pressing in on me. I miss the people, I miss the interlocutor. I will have to domesticate one of the parrots and teach it to speak.

Day 3

Like every day, I went for my morning flight this morning. But soon I had to turn the plane around and land. The engine started coughing. At first, I thought I was going to crash, but despite my lack of aviation knowledge, I managed to land. I forgot to refuel. I spent the day by plane. I have carried out a thorough check. The fuel was certainly of poorer quality due to its age, but Brian made sure it was well stored and survived.

Day 4

I spent the day wandering around outside the property. I found a large meteorite crater with a lake in it. I have never seen as many different birds as I saw there in my life. I even managed to catch some trout-like fish, which I baked for lunch. On the other bank, on the opposite side of the lake, I saw a herd of cattle drinking in the lake. I returned home before dark.

Day 5

I didn't want to get out of bed today. Loneliness, anxiety and hopelessness have cornered me. A difficult day.

Days 6, 7, 8, 9, 10, 11

I was in a mental coma for seven days. I couldn't pick myself up. I wanted to die. I no longer saw the point. I am sentenced to life imprisonment. It is all in vain.

For seven days, I was locked in the house in a semi-wakeful state. God couldn't help me either, or didn't want to. I miss Beti, my mum, Brian; I miss Rudy and Ana, Michael and Susan. I miss Karen the most. She was the last person I lived with. I hope Beti forgives me. Neither meditation, nor breathing, nor convincing myself that this is the life I must accept, nor its afterlife, helped me. Knowing that I was in prison without the possibility of a pardon made me very sad. I am breathing better as I write this. The dingoes rescued me, or rather the cattle, who were mooing loudly for help when they were attacked by dingoes. Maybe He sent the dingoes? I took my rifle and ran towards the mooing cattle. When I saw a pack of frantic dingoes coming at two calves, I fired into the air. The attackers fled. I buried the cadavers of calves in the ground and then went hunting for the dingoes that had scattered around the property. When I saw them, I fired at them. I killed three dingoes. At least, five were still alive. I had to find them. By the evening, I had killed two more. Then I checked the fence to see where they had sneaked onto the property. I found an opening that was the work of days of persistent dingoes. I fixed a leaky fence. Obviously, I will have to check the protective netting around the property on a daily basis. That night I finally slept.

Day 12

I started the day like the days before the coma. Meditation, flight and a tour of the estate. I was looking for at least three more dingoes. Everything was fine with the cattle. I found two more sheep that had been nibbled and half-eaten. Were the dingoes still on the property, or had they escaped? I was tormented by this question. I spent the whole day looking for dingoes, combing the ranch in detail. There was no trace of dingoes. I hoped they had escaped through the hole in the fence before I patched it. I had a drink in the evening.

Day 13

I calmed down. I started to breathe again. The day passed without any noteworthy events. I just want to mention that I almost cut off my left index finger when repairing a wooden tool. I managed to stop the bleeding, but the cut was wide and I had to patch it up. I started stitching awkwardly, but in the end I managed to stitch the wound somehow with three Picasso stitches. Each one was unique.

Day 14

I spent the day in the garden. I've made beds and sown and planted vegetables, which will become scarce over time; courgettes, carrots, tomatoes and beans. I chanted Namah Shivaya all day. Working and singing calmed me down completely. It was a different world, but a beautiful one. Life is beautiful. I am breathing, so I am. I am aware that the attacks of anxiety and loneliness will come, but with each passing day I will be stronger and more prepared for their attack. I had a long talk with Beti in the cemetery. She is waiting for me. Brian and Karen are waiting for me too, as are my mother and the others. "I'll come."

Day 15

I spent the whole day in the air. When I ran out of fuel, I landed, refuelled and took off again. I flew in concentric circles around Atlantis. Not a soul anywhere, except for many animals. At the furthest point, two hundred and fifty kilometres south of the ranch, I saw the wreckage of a helicopter without markings. I managed to land next to it so that I could see the accident site. I found two human skeletons in a rather overgrown, wrecked helicopter. I could make out Andy Perkovich and Amanda Johanson on the faded passports. I also found a suitcase full of US dollars. I dug the hole with a shovel I had in the plane. I put their passports and money in the pit next to the skeletons. I planted a cross on the mound on which I wrote their names. My estimate is that the wrecks were more than ten years old. Before returning to Atlantis, I wanted to land next to a very attractive lake with a waterfall, where I wanted to freshen up. Before I touched the ground, I saw a deep channel in front of me that I couldn't see from the air. I immediately put on the accelerator and pulled the wheel towards me. I managed to avoid an accident. I could have died in the crash or, injured, I could have waited for death far from the ranch. I was very careful when landing at the ranch.

Day 16

I will give the plane a few days off. Today I spent the day at the ranch with the animals. I milked a lot of milk. I decided to make some cheese wheels. I aged it in an underground warehouse, where we made special chambers for this purpose and for drying the meat, where we allowed air and smoke to flow in from the surface through pipes. We needed smoke for smoked meat or cheese. I designed the cheese wheels artistically. Each one was unique. I will be working on cheeses all week. In the evening, I fell asleep in the front yard. I drank too much brandy.

Days 17, 18, 19, 20, 21, 22

Cheese-making. I enjoyed the artistic and cheese-making freedom I allowed myself in making cheese. I also supervised what was happening in the garden. I sang all the time I was working. I made up songs and lyrics. I spontaneously became a composer and a poet.

I had too much poultry, so I pardoned many chickens, geese and ducks. I let them run free around the ranch. I found another sheep, killed not long ago and half eaten. Obviously there is at least one dingo or other animal on the property that is killing my livestock without my permission. I combed the ranch length and breadth, but found no intruder. There are more than enough sheep, cows and goats, but I could not afford a murderous intruder who could decimate my flock with his companions. I checked the fence again, but I couldn't find a hole in it.

Day 23

Keeping a diary is one of the things that fill my day. Nevertheless, I have decided to write once a week from now on. If one day something interesting happens that I have to write about, then I will break that decision. The long beard started to turn grey, and the hair also started to turn silver. Sometimes I put them in a ponytail; sometimes I let them float free, depending on what I was doing. I braided the hairs on my chin.

Week 1

In the past week, I have stocked up on meat. The garden also took me a few days. I grew everything I needed on it. I have walked a lot off the estate. Thanks to good orientation and making sure I got back in time, I had no problems wandering around. I found the remains of a weather balloon and human footprints. An abandoned old hearth, probably from the Aborigines. Are there any of them still alive? Perhaps I am not alone in this world, alongside robots and masters. For a while, I hoped to find some more clues. I found nothing more. I drank every night. Do I do drugs? Do I need a drug?

Week 2

I was woken by the low overflight of a jet. Are they looking for me? I didn't fly that day. I was distilling brandy. I put everything that was edible in the cauldron and started the fire. The brandy wasn't top-notch, but it was drinkable. I roasted a lamb on a spit in front of the house. I made myself a feast. I fell asleep to the sound by the fire. The next day I decided to be a moderate drinker. In a corner of the property where I had never been before, I found Indian hemp growing on a good part of the ranch. Did Brian used to grow cannabis? Did he smoke weed when we were together? He never told me. I was extremely happy to find it.

I won't need to drink anymore. I had marijuana in abundance. I carved a pipe out of wood and pressed cannabis into it. I always had my pipe and bag of weed with me. These days Bob Marley has been my faithful companion. I also baked cookies and made cannabis tea. Ganja rules.

Week 3

I still had occasional anxiety attacks, which I successfully fought off with weed. Some days I overdid it and was stoned from morning till night. Now I smoke it only in the evening, sometimes in between if the need arises. Tea and cookies are always available. I didn't want to make plans anymore. I kept my morning routine and then did what my inner voice told me to do. I tried to listen to it. Somehow I managed. I had days when I smoked weed on the terrace and avoided work. But there were also days when I worked like a madman. But sometimes I had to leave the farm and go into the wild. On one of my trips, a flying insect stung my arm, my forearm. I had a lower arm like Popeye for a few days. Nothing worse, thank God.

Week 4

That bite was not so innocent. Some days I was flabbier. I had a headache and felt best outside in the shade in a lying position. It's gone. I went back to my daily routine. While lying down, I thought a lot about the world that used to be. Anyone who was paying attention could see even then that things were moving in the direction of globalisation, unification, total control. I recalled an interesting conversation I had in Switzerland, a few years before I visited Geneva, when a Swiss colleague explained to me that students at the University of Bern had entered the data of thirty thousand of the world's biggest companies into a powerful computer. They had made startling discoveries. The world's thirty thousand biggest companies are owned by a few mega-corporations, but controlled by a handful of people. So the entire world economy, trading, banking, media, educational institutions, entertainment, practically everything in the world was in the hands of just a few people. They have bought and taken over companies, destroying or upgrading them. They controlled politicians, installed presidents, blackmailed monarchs, fomented wars, sold arms, shaped public opinion. They are the ones who hired the scientists who created nanotechnology and drove humanity into extinction. If they controlled everything, including food production, then they also controlled genetic changes in humans. And with nanotechnology, they have finally created a world in their image. They have always been the masters, from the first man onwards. Today's rulers are descended from the rulers of Babylon. Everything is connected, everything makes sense, everything is clear. Earth has been usurped by the dark forces of the Universe. Why does God allow this? I continued to ponder this question for a few days.

Week 5

Why does God allow it? I got an answer. It was sent to me by the Universe through the weed. The answer was free will, again, the much vaunted, free will.

Our free will, our freedom, has succumbed to the dark forces of the Universe. They made sheep from us and we wanted to become sheep. We have accepted the world as it has been drawn for us. Potemkin village. Bread and games. They have taken over religions to keep us away from the truth. They have made fools of us, and they have succeeded perfectly. Finally, we were taken to slaughter. We went voluntarily, without any hesitation. What fools, poor bastards. They controlled everything, only the human spirit was inaccessible to them, but they tamed it with a mind that accepted the knowledge they created, they invented. Scientists worked for them, even though they thought they were working for humanity. They have elevated science to the pedestal of a supreme deity, and turned religions into fairy tales for little children, run by carefully guarded mafias ordained by the devil. What a perfect script, what a superb performance. They turn the sinless into the sinful, the sinful into the sinless, without the consent of the Universe, without the consent of the Creator. Or is it?

When I was looking for articles and books about the global elite and their conspiracies before I came to Australia, I came across an article or a recorded interview with a secret member of the global elite, which was conducted via email. At the time, this interview seemed to me like a fictional story, a fairy tale, a fantastic Stephen King story, a hair-brained confession. Today, I am not sure that it is all made up. Someone who claimed to be a member of the global elite that rules the world was approached through the media. He said that interested parties could write to him with questions, to which he would reply as soon as possible. His confession was that their group, which controls everything in this world, is called Lucifer. They incite people to sin, to do wrong, to kill, to steal, to torture, to manipulate, to intimidate, and to do evil. They are the ones who rule over the entire world economy, finance, politics and religion. What is most interesting and surprising is his statement that they are only fulfilling an agreement with the Creator. They come from the positive sixth density of consciousness, even though they do negative things. They made a deal with the Creator to make life on Earth harder for people and to lure them into sin by tricks.

And only those whose free will and spirit are stronger than Lucifer will progress to the higher, positive fourth density of consciousness, and most of them will be reborn in the third dimension, in the third density of consciousness. Those who surrender completely to evil will regress to the negative fourth density, where life is much more difficult than on Earth.

Particularly interesting is his account of Jesus, who is said to be truly alive and to have come into the world from positive fifth density to help people and show them the way to progress towards the Father, the Creator. Jesus was born just like all human beings born on Earth. He lived like all the children, adolescents of that time. At the transition from childhood to adolescence, he allegedly committed a crime, killing a friend at play. He was so affected by this that he fled his home and wandered in deserts and lonely areas. That's when he realised who he really was. He knew that he had come into the world to help people find the right path in life and to encourage them to do well in the service of the Father, the Creator. His seed bore good fruit for three hundred years, but then Lucifer, through Constantine, intervened in Christianity.

Everything is connected and everything has logic. The book about terrorists and the Illuminati, what Beti told me and this forgotten interview? Beings from higher densities of consciousness have voluntarily come into the world to help humanity fight Lucifer. So the Creator has not forgotten about people. He gave them a choice, just as John Steinbeck wrote in his novel East of Eden. God has banished man from paradise, but has given him the opportunity to return if he really wants to. And he is helped in this by beings from higher densities of consciousness, but on the other hand, he is also hindered by beings from higher densities. But it is up to the individual to decide which path to choose and take. Buddha, Jesus, Saint Augustine, Mohammed, Saint Teresa of Avila, various prophets and messiahs, these were beings who helped humanity. On the other side was Lucifer.

This thinking prompted me to start reading a collection of five books that Beti left me, The Law of One, which recorded a small group of people from the United States communicating through a medium with a group of beings from the sixth density positive called Ra, who were supposed to have been among us in the time of ancient Egypt. They also helped build the pyramids, whose function was to transmit energy from outer space to the Earth for its healing, for the healing of its inhabitants. Similar pyramids were helped to be built in other parts of the world, all with the same function. Ra was the Egyptian sun god, creator of men and gods. So Ra was an entity from the sixth density of consciousness who came to help people on earth and lived among them physically, in ancient Egypt. Later, it would return to Earth, but no longer in physical form, as it did in Egypt.

Week 6

I did a lot of thinking, pondering and painting pictures in my head. I was working, flying, walking, but my head was always in the stratosphere. All these theories and thinking about them gave me a new impetus and will to live. I forgot about loneliness because I was socialising with beings from higher dimensions, from higher levels of density of consciousness.

"I'll do my job," I told myself as my energy and willpower ran out. I have lived in two worlds. I was working on Earth and my thoughts and prayers were drifting up to the heights where I wanted to go. I was ready for a repeat of the third density, but at the same time I was convinced that I could not go backwards. I have never knowingly wished or done anything bad to anyone in my life. I was looking at pictures and records of my life, taking stock of it. Is this done before death?

I wake up in the morning and everything that yesterday I accepted as sacred and found logic and validation, today has turned to rubbish. It was all nonsense, far-fetched. How is this possible? Or does my mind constantly remind me that I have gone astray. But then what is the point if all what is written and all thinking about is just rubbish. Why always doubt? Why always weighing? When you put a thought or a thesis on the scales, the mind goes to the opposite side and pulls with all its might towards the ground. Into reality? Either the mind knows everything, or it knows nothing and plays its own game. Whose game? He is obviously playing a game that he has adopted from those who have given it knowledge, which is not really knowledge. What is knowledge? Is it information someone has given you, or is it your own experience? So the earth is not round and does not orbit the sun because I do not have this experience? How to tell the wheat from the chaff? What is real knowledge, what is 'false' information? Why am I banging my head? There are things, knowledge, which is passed down from generation to generation. Some things cannot be denied or falsified by the masters. Were they the ones who drove out science in the Middle Ages through the Christian Church? Then, when there was no other way out, they adopted it and made it their own. They adopted the renaissance, humanism and the enlightenment. They had led revolutions. They were against Christianity, even though they themselves had transformed it into their own image. They have always been on the winning side because they have always been on both sides. Win, win position.

And then I came to faith again. Believe it or not. You believe in what you can touch, not with your fingers, but with your heart.

I have won, I believe and I believe because I feel so. The plus has overcome the minus; although there would be no plus if there were no minus. Negative forces can affect the way of thinking of an individual at the level of consciousness. They send their signals into my consciousness. The positive forces are sending their own. I decide which signals to give priority to. Does that make me a winner or a loser? In any case, a winner! Is it?

Week 7 and Some More Weeks or Even Months

After careful and painstaking reconsideration, I will write only when I feel like it. I can't write anymore. The work was my prayer and my writing. Through my work, the spirit took over. The mind has accepted the partnership and at the same time, the superiority of the spirit. I have tried to live in their harmony. I am slowly making progress. The path is difficult. I insist.

I stopped drinking alcohol. I kept the marijuana for a friend. I have had few encounters with the mirror. In the mirror, I saw Robinson, the castaway, Tom Hanks without Wilson, a ragged man dressed in torn and dirty clothes. I washed out of necessity, not out of habit. I ate when I was hungry. I didn't think or worry about when breakfast, lunch or dinner would be. I have not even named these meals with these names anymore. My morning meditations were getting longer and longer, even my plane flights were a meditation. My work is meditation, my wanderings are meditation. I meditate, so I am. Am I leaving this world already? I don't know. I will definitely go. I'll be ready to go in a little while. I'll fly away among the stars, to Beti and Mum. Everyone is waiting for me there. They will probably give me a reception banquet when I come to see them. The prodigal son is back. When I leave earth, I will turn off the light. Maybe I will return to it one day, as a lord, as Lucifer, or as a wanderer who will come to help people, if they ever live on this planet again. Maybe on a similar planet. The Earth will be recycled; Lucifer will have done his job. "The winner takes it all." Who will be the winner?

10

I am writing, so I am. I don't know how many times the sun has risen since the last record. What I am writing now happened a few days ago. I have to put down on paper what I experienced that evening and what I have been reliving for days afterwards. When I returned home from a wander around the ranch, I was lost in memories of my mother and Beti. I get to the house and hear human voices inside. I approach the door and I can clearly hear my mother and Beti talking. What the fuck. Am I crazy? Too much weed? I also sipped some wine that day. Beti and Mum?

"Beti, don't hold it against David that he was with Karen…"

"I don't blame him, they were both lonely. Brian and I died and they were left alone. They became close in a purely human way. Maybe the same would have happened to Brian and me if we had stayed alive."

"On earth, everything is completely different from where we are. We are all together all the time, we are all one, but on earth, every man is for himself. We do not know jealousy, envy, hatred, greed, bloodthirstiness, lies, and while on earth, everyone fights for himself, kidnaps and owns another human being. Here on earth, not everyone can love each other, each with each, one with all, but only two can love each other. They are divided into genders, into nations, into skin colours, each with his own god. They do not realise that they are all one, they come from one and they return to one. It is that simple, but the seed of doubt about eternity and oneness makes people egoistic creatures who think that everything begins and will end in this world they live in. If people knew what real life is like, they would not cling so tightly to this life on earth, which is just the beginning of a long journey. Already in this world, they should be thinking about what awaits them after their earthly life. But man succumbs to too many pitfalls hidden in everyday life. And on top of it all, money has replaced the Creator. Well, that's over now. Some of them felt the truth in their lifetime, some of them just before they died, and some of them persevered to the end."

"David has succeeded. Even when I was with him on earth, I was convinced of that. He always knew; he always suspected; that there was something out there, something much bigger than life on earth. He, like all people, was always fighting his own mind, the demons, and the devil's emissaries, who convinced him that there is no life after life."

"When he knows who he really is, he will remember why he came into the world. He saved many people. Now he is saving himself."

Am I mad? Auditory hallucinations? Or…I went into the house and there was no one there. There was no Beti, there was no Mum. But I heard them so clearly and distinctly. Did the message come from there? Was that conversation what I have heard meant to encourage me not to give up, to hold on for as long as I am meant to? Was it too much weed again?

11

Days, months pass. I think it's been more than three years or more since the day Karen said goodbye. I look more and more like a castaway. I have hair almost down to my buttocks and a beard down to my belly button. I work as much as necessary to survive. I talk to Him all day long. Many things are clear to me, many things are not. I will probably clarify this in my next life. There are fewer and fewer battles with myself. I'm breathing. I don't think about death anymore. I will be ready when it arrives.

One morning, as I was talking to the sun, I heard human voices, or so it seemed to me. Maybe it's Beti and Stanka wandering around the ranch again, or even Brian and Karen, I thought. And then the voices grew louder and more intense. I became agitated. I took my rifle and left Atlantis. I spent the whole day poking around, but I didn't meet a single person, I didn't find a single clue to confirm my suspicions. Either I have become an antenna for voices from beyond the earth, or I have shrunk my brain by hyper-consumption of cannabis. That night I dreamt that Atlantis was some kind of amusement park, a reality show, an open-air museum, and that robots were coming to watch me. And they were amused to see the hairy creature that is supposed to be their ancestor. The robots made fun of the last man on earth and competed to see who could come up with the most jokes at my expense. When I woke up in the morning, I remembered the dream vividly and in detail. Are they really watching me, I thought. Am I really their monkey, a kangaroo, or maybe a cockatoo? Or I'm an Australian woodland creature, a Yeti, a Bigfoot? Over the next few days, I searched for clues about the mysterious visitors in the wider area around the ranch, but to no avail. I found nothing. Then, a few weeks later, I found a strange device near Atlantis. It was like a mobile phone, but without a screen. The discovery was very upsetting and took away my daily peace. I fell asleep in the evening with anxiety in my heart and woke up the next day with the same anxiety. I was observing a device I found that was without the necessary power supply. Useless, but what was it for? I thought it was a holographic phone or something. I spent my days outside the estate. I was looking for further clues about uninvited visitors. I found nothing more. After three or four months of excitement, I returned to my routine and the peace I had created for myself.

12

I gathered enough strength to take my notebook out of my trouser pocket, where I wrote down everything the masters of my body told me to do. I haven't touched a pencil for a few months. I don't know, maybe even twelve or more, I didn't count. But it didn't matter either. I couldn't write. I had no need to write. I have written down what I had to say. I lived between heaven and earth. The body was on the ranch, the spirit was in space. I survived until today.

I woke up in a wrecked plane. How long I was asleep or unconscious, I don't know. Everything was strange, foggy, and unreal. I remembered that I was flying, circling over the ranch, and then something rattled. I've been hit by a drone or run over by a bird or flock of birds. I could no longer control it. It flew up and down, left and right, always contrary to what I wanted. The rudder did not obey. Before the darkness overtook me, I remember that I was flying towards the houses. Then there was a boom and darkness. When I woke up, my chest was wedged between the handlebars and the seat. Blood was coming out of my ears and I was spitting blood out of my mouth. My legs were dead. The left arm was apparently broken or at least fractured. The right one was fine. With the strength I gathered through concentration, I managed to move my upper body. I got out of my armour. I couldn't rely on my legs as if I didn't have them. I managed to open the door and fall out of the plane onto the ground. The pain was indescribable. I tried to forget about it. I lay on the floor for a while. Then, with great effort, I started to crawl. Useless legs with open fractures, possibly a damaged spine, a semi-useful left and a useful right arm. Mission impossible. Every movement of the body was torture. I needed a longer rest every two or three moves. It didn't work. The houses were three or four hundred metres away. I will not succeed. I lost consciousness. When I came to myself, I resumed my journey, my way of the cross, my Calvary. I had more than fourteen stations. I was sure that was the end of it. In fact, I knew that my departure time had come. I was spitting blood; blood was coming out of my legs. I left a trail of blood behind me. Cows, bulls, sheep, goats, chickens, geese, ducks came to me, birds flew over me. As if the animals knew that this is the last path of the last free man. That's why they followed me. I lost consciousness again. When I opened my eyes, a young goat was licking my mouth. I was thirsty, terribly thirsty. So I veered slightly off the straight line and crawled up to the pool where the animals were drinking water. The water saved me from dying there on the lawn. I had to get to the houses, although I don't know what the point of the torture was. There was no solution for me anyway. More and more blood was pooling in my mouth, probably also gushed in my body due to internal bleeding. My mind told me to stop, you have no chance. I agreed with it. But the spirit persisted and dragged me across the meadow.

My mother was there with Beti. They were the two who accompanied me and encouraged me. Unconsciousness again, darkness. When I came to myself, I pulled myself forward. Night has fallen. "Last night?" I wondered. Will I live to see the morning? What the morning means to me. I fell asleep halfway. I dreamt that everyone was waiting for me at a party. When they saw me, they were extremely happy and patted me on the back. There was Mum, Brian, Anna, Rudi, Michael, Susan, Kamala, Joseph, Dr Kendall, Monica, Vasili, Sarrah, Marghrete, all friends and acquaintances. Beti and Karen were both dressed in white. Both were brides. I thought Brian and I were getting married together. But I was the groom and they were my brides. My mother was the priestess who married us. Brian was the first to congratulate me, telling me that he had married both of them before I arrived. Then we continued to marry each other, men to men, women to women. We were all intertwined and we were all married. We were all one. I thought I was already there, but then the cow's tongue made me come out of my sleep.

When I woke up, it was still dark, with only a glimmer in the east, but my direction was west. After the toilet, breakfast and meditation, I'm kidding, I continued my journey. My faithful friends were with me all night and they continued to be with me. Now and then I have been treated to the saliva of a cow, a sheep or a goat. That was the only liquid I got. I was trying to relieve my pain with weed, but I lost it somewhere with my pipe.

My last journey is not over yet. I crawled on my belly all day. I suffered a lot. Is this my last payment before I go upstairs, I wondered. Beti and my mother were always encouraging me. And the animals made sure I didn't bleed out and get dehydrated. Their saliva stopped the bleeding on my legs and gave me much-needed fluids in very small quantities. There was also less blood in my mouth. Had the bleeding stopped?

In the evening, I dragged myself to the cemetery with the last of my strength. I couldn't manage an inch more. I fell asleep. At night, they all came to visit me again. Beti and my mother nursed me back to health and all my wounds healed instantly. Then we all hugged and danced. We didn't talk at all, we communicated only telepathically, with our thoughts. Love, love everywhere and understanding. It was beautiful. I was woken up by the cow's tongue again. Wasn't that my last night?

Then I wanted to get to the houses, to the water. It didn't work. The water was too far away. I remembered the two vases of flowers I had brought to the graves of Beti and Karen before I took the last flight. First, I crawled with great difficulty to the grave where Karen was lying. The water was green and already smelled of rot. But it was water. I drank it. I wanted more. Somehow I managed to roll away onto Beti's grave. I'll drink more of this water, I thought, and then maybe I'll manage to drag myself to the house where I'll meet my death. When I reached for the vase, I knocked it over with my limp hand. Water spilled on the dry soil. I wanted to roll over on my back and cry. I rolled from the mound into the grave next to it, which I dug for myself. My coffin was already in it. That ended and sealed my path. There was no way I could get out of the grave. I found it tragicomic that I managed to reach my own grave. OK, I'm going to die here. Appropriately. I felt nothing anymore, no pain, not even my body. I felt a notebook and a pen in my trouser pocket. I half sat down and leaned against the headboard of the coffin. I don't know how, but I did it. I managed to take a pencil in my trembling right hand and write down what had happened in my notebook. It flew out of me, but my hand couldn't follow the thoughts that wanted to go on paper. Nevertheless, I have written everything down.

Then I rested and waited. Well, I did not rest, I suffered. I was barely alive, lying in a coffin in a grave I dug for myself.

I have had another morning. I am sure it is the last. It was a terrible night. I was in pain again, spitting blood, burning in my mouth and throat. I was thirsty, terribly thirsty. Something was biting my legs and licking the blood that was slowly oozing from the open wounds. Whether they were rats or other animals, I don't know. There was nothing I could do. I can still move my arms. I was reminded of the passage in the Bible where Jesus asked the Creator before He died. I don't know how or where it got into my head and on through my right hand and pen to paper. I am not a Bible scholar, but this phrase is completely familiar to me, as if I had lived with it all my life:

"Father, if you will, take this cup of suffering away from me. Not my will, however, but your will be done."

I'm still writing; I want to write…I can't take it anymore. I'm just laughing…I am laughing because I am finally going.

I will put the booklet in a plastic bag that I have with me. Maybe someone will find it one day.

Goodbye Atlantis.

Beti, can you hear me? I come to you. Adonai.